It was all set to go to hell

In the next few heartbeats, the soldier veered a few steps across the floor, hosing the cockpit with a long burst of autofire.

The Executioner's sweeping gunfire drilled a few wild rounds into the instrument panel, sent sparks flying around the cockpit, while still more streaks of blood hit the Plexiglas. The copilot jumped from his seat only to start dancing around as the lead tumblers chopped him up. He was toppling over the control panel, sliding down over the throttle, when his convulsing death throes began hitting the control sticks, pitching the chopper.

The floor was leaning up before Bolan, but he was already racing for the door. On the fly, the soldier leaped out the doorway, sailed a few feet to a hard landing. Catching his balance, the soldier pivoted and tapped the M-203's trigger.

This was one bird he didn't want to see rise again.

MACK BOLAN ®
The Executioner

DON PENDLETON'S

EXECUTIONER®
STEALTH STRIKER

A GOLD EAGLE BOOK FROM

WORLDWIDE®

TORONTO • NEW YORK • LONDON
AMSTERDAM • PARIS • SYDNEY • HAMBURG
STOCKHOLM • ATHENS • TOKYO • MILAN
MADRID • WARSAW • BUDAPEST • AUCKLAND

First edition July 2001
ISBN 0-373-64272-5

Special thanks and acknowledgment to
Dan Schmidt for his contribution to this work.

STEALTH STRIKER

Printed in U.S.A.

The human mind is our fundamental resource.
                                    —John F. Kennedy

A fanatic is one who can't change his mind and won't
change the subject.
                                    —Winston Churchill

A scientist without ethics is the most menacing threat.
Science must have the freedom to discover but only
for the good of the people, not at the expense of lives.
                                    —Mack Bolan

THE
MACK BOLAN®
LEGEND

Nothing less than a war could have fashioned the destiny of the man called Mack Bolan. Bolan earned the Executioner title in the jungle hell of Vietnam.

But this soldier also wore another name—Sergeant Mercy. He was so tagged because of the compassion he showed to wounded comrades-in-arms and Vietnamese civilians.

Mack Bolan's second tour of duty ended prematurely when he was given emergency leave to return home and bury his family, victims of the Mob. Then he declared a one-man war against the Mafia.

He confronted the Families head-on from coast to coast, and soon a hope of victory began to appear. But Bolan had broken society's every rule. That same society started gunning for this elusive warrior—to no avail.

So Bolan was offered amnesty to work within the system against terrorism. This time, as an employee of Uncle Sam, Bolan became Colonel John Phoenix. With a command center at Stony Man Farm in Virginia, he and his new allies—Able Team and Phoenix Force—waged relentless war on a new adversary: the KGB.

But when his one true love, April Rose, died at the hands of the Soviet terror machine, Bolan severed all ties with Establishment authority.

Now, after a lengthy lone-wolf struggle and much soul-searching, the Executioner has agreed to enter an "arm's-length" alliance with his government once more, reserving the right to pursue personal missions in his Everlasting War.

PROLOGUE

He was running for his life, but his tired, stumbling pace fell short of the hard charge he so desperately needed.

Three sets of potential dire straits, he knew, could abort his break for freedom any second, leave him sprawled and heaving, or convulsing in death throes on the desert floor. His first liability was a soft and flabby body. The heaviest thing he'd lifted in years was a petri dish; the hardest exercise he'd known in recent memory was lumbering around and sweating his ass off in a Nuclear Biological Chemical—NBC—decontamination suit. Any second now he dreaded the sharp pains in his left arm and chest that would drop him on his knees, the agony and shortness of breath signaling the onslaught of yet another heart attack.

His second problem, also potentially fatal, was snakes. This stretch of southwest Utah was notorious for western rattlesnakes. The serpents came out primarily at night when the desert cooled off and they could hunt for prey, unseen, drawn, he believed, to body heat. Some of the venomous predators were rumored as long as ten feet, a few of those slithering coils of reptilian anger thicker than a baseball bat, or so the stories went. Supposedly their bite wasn't often fatal, but he wasn't about to believe the first word that came out of his superiors' mouths, not after what he knew, what he'd seen. No sir, not anymore, he thought, take your former rank and current civilian stature and shove it. From where he'd just escaped truth, justice and the American way were clearly open to a sinister interpretation.

With his mind eaten up by terror and agitation, he began seeing shadows crawling all over the ground, sliding toward him, coiling up from all directions, dripping fangs glistening against the moonlight. Or was it just a shadow cast by a cloud moving beneath the moon? Or his imagination inflamed by terror, eyes seeing something that wasn't there? Whatever, given his age, blood pressure that was off the meter—not to mention two recent heart attacks and his present state of near exhaustion—he could be sure that, once bitten, he'd stay down for the count.

And Jonathan Randall imagined himself a human sauna at the moment, his body throwing off enough heat to draw a few curious rattlers his way. What was that shadow on the ground, dead ahead, writhing near some tumbleweed? Choking down a startled cry, he veered around it, cursing the wall of darkness shrouding his unseen terrors, whether real or imagined.

The desert all around him was black despite a soft sheen of light twinkling from the countless stars above, the sky, broken here and there by a scuttling cloud bank. Even more awful, the full moon seemed to demand the occasional howl of a coyote, that particular eerie cry from some invisible beast baying at the heavens only tweaking his nerves more. At least the penlight he wielded helped steer him some as he wheezed and weaved his way past sagebrush and juniper, or trudged up the rock-littered spines of arroyos and gullies.

He searched the broken ground ahead, embarked on a tentative march into yet another gully on his uphill climb, his light flicking on and off. He stumbled suddenly. Pitched to the earth, he inhaled a mouthful of dust as he sucked in air. Then he cursed the loud rasping in his ears, his burning lungs starved for oxygen, heart pounding like a jackhammer in the tight coil of his chest. It was damn cold out there, but he was still clammy with sweat that seemed to chill him only more to the bone. Somehow he heaved himself standing, hacking out the grit, but wondered how much more fear he could dredge up just to keep his legs moving. He listened to his choked breathing for a moment, tried to control his intake of air while he fought to clear his throat and lungs of dust. He checked the jagged plateau to the north. Sound carried a long way in the desert. So did light. But if *they* could hear and see him, he should be able to make out their approach, right?

If he could hear them coming, he knew it would be all over but the begging for his life to be spared.

And it was dire straits number three that prevented him from keeping the pencil-thin beam on for any longer than a two- or three-second stretch to help guide him. The last, but certainly not least of his worries, were the black helicopters. Any second he feared those grim and silent Men in Black, armed with automatic weapons, would mow him down where he stood. He could be sure, given what he'd done to break out of the installation, and what he knew, they would shoot first. And no one would bother with questions, even after the fact.

It was that one subtle, between-the-lines clause in the contract he'd signed with them, a little over one year ago when he was recruited out of Fort Detrick. Defensive biological-chemical warfare studies and research, his ass. The bottom line, the escape hatch on their end to his contract, he knew, was that dead men told no tales, revealed no secrets.

He was topping the gully, stumbling on, when he slammed into something that knocked him to his knees, snapped the air from his lungs. His first thought was that the Men in Black had intercepted him, that he was finished. He was shaking, strangling down the cry of alarm, when he looked up and found he'd slammed into a large wooden board, impaled by metal stakes into the ground. No MIBs, thank God. He grasped the plywood board's edge, flicked on the penlight—and nearly laughed out loud at what he read on the other side.

Warning. Property Of United States Government. Area Contaminated By Anthrax. Forbidden To Pass Beyond This Point.

The absurdity, no, the audacity of that claim finally brought a grim chuckle from his parched mouth. Then the clincher.

Use Of Deadly Force Authorized.

That much was true, he thought. They could do anything to anybody they wanted and get away with it. The anthrax angle was a smoke screen, at least as far as any anthrax spores poisoning the surrounding desert. The insidious proclamation was meant to drive away the curious, the thrill-seekers with too much time and imagination on their hands.

But he knew the truth, and it was far more horrible than some anthrax scare. In fact, there were two floppy disks he'd lifted from his office, stashed now in the pocket of his windbreaker. If he could get what was on those disks to someone in the outside world, maybe the FBI, the Justice Department...

But where was he going to run? He took a moment to get his bearings, figuring he'd put at least two miles to the installation, hopefully more. No black helicopters swarmed the skies yet, which told him they hadn't bypassed the lockdown code. Their own culture of arrogance had allowed him to nearly walk out the front door. Now they were trapped inside, engineers scrambled, Major Paxson snarling out his anger, most likely, while they fought like hell to splice together the right wires.

No time to gloat on how he'd outsmarted them. He was far from any finish line.

Okay, he had a rough mental lay of the land. When he'd been choppered in from Nellis Air Force Base, the desert was an empty lunar landscape for as far as the eye could see. By night it was the dark side of the moon. Then there was the makeshift R and R complex, a small prefab town, complete with all the creature comforts and amenities, recently built by the Army for various government employees, military types with the highest security clearances available. They were a mixed civilian-military populace from Wendover Range, Dugway Proving Grounds, the Desert Range Experimental Station, all of them living together while they were under contract to the government or military.

But now Compound Camellion—how aptly named, he thought—was out of the question. One, he was moving in the wrong direction, couldn't risk backtracking. Second, the minicity on the desert was always crawling with MIBs, infiltrated among the workforce to silence any shoptalk over a cold beer. Cedar City, he believed, was probably forty, fifty miles tops, due southeast, and offered the only closest airport he could think of. But he would never make it there on foot, not before he was snatched up anyway. A motel with a phone—that was the answer. But where? And he had no money.

Penlight scanning the terrain ahead, and he couldn't believe he had reached a level stretch. No crags, gullies, nothing but flat, beautiful ground. Suddenly he heard the tambourine-like sound strike the air, so close he nearly screamed. He was up and running, pumping his legs, cold terror fueling his sprint. His thoughts jumbled into a silent scream as images of snakes, fully armed black helicopters, MIBs and their blazing automatic weapons meshed together, so vivid in his mind he could almost reach out and touch the mental pictures. As much as he wanted, needed to, he knew he couldn't keep up the hard run, his chest now heaving, legs on fire, but he trudged on.

No choice if he wanted to live.

Under the strain, with sweat burning into his eyes, he couldn't trust his senses, but he thought he glimpsed some black object rolling up on his left. A glance in that direction…

Oh, no, it was a vehicle, but with the headlights

out, he couldn't tell what it was exactly. Oh, God, his mind roared, they had found him.

He was a dead man.

His legs finally gave out, despair and terror helping to take him down, his body folding beneath him like melting rubber. He was nose-diving, face bouncing off the edges of rock and stone, when the vehicle skidded up and stopped less than three feet from his sprawled body. Exhaust fumes and dust choked his lungs. Gagging, he rolled up on his side, heard a door open and slam. He waited for the inevitable, braced for bullets to tear into his body, knew he would find no mercy, no waffling on their part for even the most believable of lies or excuses.

"Hey, are you all right, mister?"

Through a misty veil, he stared up at the shadow, his eyes teared by sweat. No gun that he could make out, but there were some type of goggles the shadow was stripping off its eyes. A harder search, the shadow repeating the question, and he made out the voice belonging to a woman. A hundred questions raced into his mind.

"Who are you?" he cried. "Are you a civilian? Are you one of them?"

The shadow hesitated. "One of who?"

A long moment of terrible silence. He lay on the ground, uncertain of everything, then cringed as she bent and grasped his shoulders. He allowed himself to be hauled to his feet.

"I saw you running from that place, whatever it really is. I thought you might need help."

"Answer me!" he barked, surprised by his own sudden anger.

She stepped back. "My name is Sally Simpson. Yes, I'm a civilian. I'm not looking to cause you any trouble, and I'm not one of 'them,' whoever they are. Please, calm down."

He searched the sky, the dark land to the north, anything but calm. "I need to get to a phone. I need a motel, someplace safe to hide," he told her, the words flooding out on a new rush of fear. "I don't have any money...."

She paused, then quietly said, "Come on, get in. I'll help you."

Help him? Why? He didn't budge as she started for the driver's door. "Why are you out here?"

She hesitated again, then answered, "I'm...trying to find out what is going on out here, that place I saw you running from."

"Why? Are you some kind of reporter?"

She grunted, displaying some fire he suddenly wished to God he possessed. "I used to be," she said. "If you can call the crap I wrote for the tabloids reporting."

"You're looking for a story?" he asked, incredulous.

"Let's just say I'm looking for the truth."

"And you think the truth is out here."

"I don't know. Maybe you can tell me."

Whatever. There was no more time for stalling. They would bypass lockdown eventually, scramble the choppers, and they wouldn't send out any search-and-rescue team. He moved for the passenger door, some type of SUV. Again he checked the sky, the black lunar terrain to the north. Nothing—yet. He jumped onto the seat, so exhausted but pumped on fear he felt as if he were slogging his way through a dream. He looked at the woman as she took the wheel, threw the goggles on the back seat. No overhead light had flashed on, which would not only allow him to make out her features, but might provide a small homing beacon on the vehicle for any watching eyes. She was a slick one, he decided, seemed to know all the right defensive, evasive moves.

"What are those?" he asked, tentative, jerking a sideways nod toward the back seat.

"Night-vision goggles. Courtesy of my ex-husband," she said, dropping the SUV into Drive. "He was in the military. Army. After the divorce he left the house in such a rush...well, he grabbed up most of the money but forgot to take a few of his toys.

"Buckle up. This dirt trail is pretty ugly for the next ten miles or so." She turned on the headlights, going against the grain for any evasive action, then gunned the engine, launching them on. "I know, it should be lights out. But their choppers are still grounded, and I don't feel like putting pedal to the metal in this terrain without being able to see what's ahead. I get the feeling somehow you locked them in." Another short silence, then she asked, "What's your name?"

He needed distance, craved safe haven. He snapped the seat belt around his chest, ignoring her question for a moment. There was a softness, a sincerity to her voice, and he wanted to believe in her—someone, anybody, for that matter—who could take him safely away from the vision of hell he'd just fled.

"Jonathan Randall. I need to know right this second, can I trust you?"

He waited as she searched his face, the SUV bounding through a rut. She nodded. "Yes."

"Simple as that?"

"Simple as that."

He looked all around the dark land, searching, fearing the sudden arrival of the black helicopters. "I need to contact someone in...law enforcement, I don't know...FBI, whatever."

"I have a source inside the Justice Department."

He looked at her. "Really?"

"Hey, I told you, I was a reporter. I've got a track record that goes beyond stories about some trailer trash impregnated by aliens."

He nodded, dubious. "Right. Okay. So, now what are you?"

"Freelance journalist."

Just his luck, he thought, stuck with someone looking for a story. If she was even who she claimed to be. "Please take me to a phone, but I told you, I don't have any money on me."

"Forget money. I have a calling card and credit cards. There's a motel I know, just the other side of Lund. I'll have to be the one who makes the call. My source at Justice might be leery of a strange voice." She must have read his suspicion, reporter's instinct for human nature flaring up. "If you want, you can listen when I put in the call. Hey, I am who I say I am."

"I suppose I'll have to trust you, Ms. Simpson. I don't see where I have a choice."

"You can call me Sally. And any time you feel you can't trust me..."

She let it hang, the woman cool and collected, but he read between the lines. Sure, he could abandon this ride at any time, brush off this stroke of luck, take his chances. No way, he decided, not on his life.

Soon enough the black helicopters would lift off, he knew, and the military men would come hunting. With all the uncertainty he faced, he knew the only one certainty was sudden death if they found him. And now there was the woman, a civilian involved in his mess. At some point very soon, he would have to tell her the facts, and let her decide if her life was worth the pursuit of truth. My God, he thought, if she only knew.

If the country only knew.

LOCKDOWN.

Under any circumstances, the dreaded word meant disaster. At the moment, it was worse than a fiasco; lockdown could mean total exposure to the outside world, unravel the project and signal his own personal apocalypse.

Roger Paxson paced around the engineer detail, silently cursing them for being so slow to find the right wires to bypass lockdown. Of course, it appeared a damn tough job at first glance, trial and error, fumbling around, all of it clearly guesswork. Talk about manual override—there looked to be a million and one wires to him, and no one on-site knew precisely which wires to connect to open the steel wall. Thanks to their escapee who had seen fit to delete the wiring hookup from the classified code file. Well, soon enough, he would find that little bastard....

If it wasn't too late.

He cracked his knuckles, growled at the trio of men in white coats, "How much longer?"

Wilson shook his head. "Hard to say, sir. When the lockdown code was installed—"

"How much longer!" he interrupted.

"Ten, maybe twenty minutes."

"You have five minutes. Anything short of that is unacceptable, and I'll hold you personally accountable."

Paxson checked his chronometer. Thirty-six minutes the guy had been on the run. He felt his rage and anxiety mount with each agonizing tick of the clock.

He paced some more, wheeling this way and that. Fear made him feel light on the feet of his six-foot-two, one-seventy frame. He was lean and mean anyway, being former Delta Force; the chiseled body beneath his black turtleneck and matching slacks was the sculpted product of some of the toughest training on earth. He found his thoughts slipping off into more-pleasant situations, all the times when that body made women swoon, melt to their knees. He snapped back, no time now to quash his fear with fantasy. He wanted to do something, anything to break out of this hole in the mountain. By God, he was also a fifth-degree black belt. A master of several styles of martial arts, his hands could snap through a dozen two-by-fours or an equal number of cinderblocks. He had cracked men's necks and backs in the lower Americas during the hunt for Noriega, crushed the bones of men in Iraq and other Gulf countries. He was focusing his rage on all those bare-hand kills, as if mental energy alone would free them all, get them moving.

A goddamn wall was about to beat him, ex-Major Roger Paxson, former commander of Delta Black Ops One Talon, the single toughest SOB to ever walk through the valley of death.

Viciously he cursed out loud, then stared with eyes like drill bits at the steel wall. No ordinary barrier by any stretch, it was eighteen inches of titanium-coated steel, now sealed up tight. Capable of being hermetically sealed under his own doomsday scenario, it was built right into the mountain, going back thirty yards in both directions.

Sure, he might be able to bench-press 450. Yes, he could hike over forty-five miles of mountainous terrain, carrying an eighty-pound load, in twenty hours. He could clear out any bar, one man, two fists and grab a brew on the way out the door with the carnage piled and whimpering all around. Been there, done all that. But being tough wouldn't beat this wall, which was built to withstand anything short of a direct nuclear hit. Of course, if the bombs started falling on the mountain, they were all finished anyway, he knew, everyone buried beneath countless tons of rock and warped steel, the lucky ones going out during the initial cave-in.

Well, the big one had just dropped—in the form of one little scientist, packing all the megatonnage in the world, in less than an ounce, he figured, of computer disks.

Pivoting in his combat boots, he stared at still more white coats. Two medics were lifting Corporal Meadows onto a gurney. The sentry's face was a lopsided swollen balloon, Meadows stirring now with a pitiful-sounding moan. Paxson had been informed by one of the medics that Meadows's pulse was weak, his jaw shattered to the point that he might need reconstructive plastic surgery. Right. If Meadows came around, Paxson might whack him another one with the wrench, but upside his skull this time.

As they wheeled Meadows off to the infirmary, Paxson kicked the HK MP-5 subgun after the stretcher. The SMG had sure proved useless in the guy's hands. Bending at the knees, he picked up the weapon used by the scientist. The wrench was heavy, maybe two pounds in his hand. Incredible, he thought, hefting the instrument of his own potential personal doom. A damn scientist had just strolled right up to Meadows and taken him out, one shot to the jaw. A swipe of his magnetic card, then punching in the classified code for lockdown.

A done deal? No way.

Paxson dropped the wrench on the steel floor, glanced over his shoulder to check on progress, but found only Wilson flinching at the heavy clang of metal on metal.

A hundred different fears and worst-case scenarios were ripping up his thoughts. Initial reports were bad enough. Randall had made off with two critical work disks. Paxson had inventory taken on a daily basis, the work in the lab reviewed by his own team of CBW specialists. Research was logged on disk. It had to be, if they were going to remember and correct any errors along the way to the various recombinant DNA.

Those disks, he knew, stored computer graphics of molecular breakdowns for some of the deadliest—

He gnashed his teeth, trying to cut short all the speculation as he ran long fingers through his black hair. If those disks fell into the hands of someone in the civilian world, hell, he knew a high-school chemistry professor, driven by the right amount of curiosity, would be able to add two and two.

Paxson suddenly saw Carl Hamilton stride through the parting steel doors of level one. He waited in the murky white light that shone from the bulbs built into both sides of the steel walls. Paxson didn't like the worried look on Hamilton's square face, the buzz cut and black clothing lending the former Delta Force captain all the grim visage of the Reaper.

"Report."

Hamilton cleared his throat. "Markinson and Axler, sir, were—how should I say?—asleep at the helm." He glanced up at the security camera monitoring the wall with ice-blue eyes. "While all this was going down, one of them apparently had his nose buried in a dirty magazine, the other one on coffee break."

Paxson felt his fury reaching critical mass. "Before they're shipped out, I will debrief and thoroughly fucking reprimand them. Their asses belong to me."

"I understand, sir."

"Do you? Randall made off with two disks that could have us shut down, and worse, if they fall into the wrong hands. He hacked into our classified files. God only knows what he's absconded with, or what he intends to do, or who he intends to take all of it to."

"He did have level-four security clearance, sir."

"Meaning?"

"Pretty much free rein. And besides, don't you think we can cover ourselves in the event of exposure?"

"I know all about who is funding us here, Captain, but those people would simply deny any involvement with this installation and the project. The same clause that is in every worker's contract here also applies to us."

Hamilton's gaze narrowed, his eyes shifting away from Paxson's penetrating dark stare. "If I may, sir?"

"What? Say it!"

"Well, it was on your orders that the night security detail was pulled in."

Paxson nodded. "True enough. There's been too many civilians traipsing around the perimeter, with their cameras and binoculars. I didn't want the choppers and men out there at night, fair game for the curious eyes of all the little people or some reporter. Obviously the posted signs warning about anthrax have only made matters worse. Two items, both judgment calls, bad ones, I admit, but that's going to change. In the morning, have the anthrax signs removed. And we fall back to full nighttime surveillance, with shoot-on-sight orders. One more thing. Not a word, not a whisper of a rumor about what happened here is to reach the rest of the work detail. Randall is on R and R in Camellion, if anyone pushes the matter."

"Understood, sir."

"Shifting gears, how is the recruiting search going?"

Paxson watched Hamilton closely, but saw no visible reaction to his mention of the search for test subjects. It was a highly sensitive matter, one that, if found out, could land all of them in Leavenworth for three hundred years.

"We're combing files now, sir. Everything from FBI files, DEA, Marshals, IRS—well, you know the drill. I believe we've found some suitable material in Los Angeles."

"Bring it here."

Now Paxson spotted the flicker of discomfort in Hamilton's eyes.

"Consider it done, sir." Hamilton cleared his throat. "May I say something?"

"What?"

"I believe the experiments, sir, are causing some unease among the workforce. They're civs, for the most part, they have no true grasp of the larger picture."

"Is that right? Well, from here on, Captain, watch everyone closely, and I'm putting you personally in charge of that particular spy detail. Any malcontents among the ranks, I want them smelled out and brought to me. Potential troublemakers will be reread their contracts. I feel out any more Randalls...well, it's a big desert out there, Captain. I'm not opposed to spreading around a little human fertilizer."

He looked at his watch before the dark expression dropped over Hamilton's face. "Wilson! How much longer?"

"I think we've almost got it, sir. This combination—"

"Save it! You're on the clock, mister. I'm looking at two minutes and fifteen seconds and counting."

Paxson brushed past Hamilton. He needed a moment alone, to think, to dread the future if those doors didn't part.

"I'VE SEEN the signs warning about anthrax."

Randall was searching the darkness beyond their motel room when he heard the woman speak. Their room was at the far edge of a place that didn't even have a name—just Motel on the board hanging from the office. Besides the woman's Jeep Cherokee, there were a few other vehicles—pickup trucks, a Harley-Davidson—parked near their window. At the end of the dirt strip leading to the motel he watched a shadow walking around the combo gas station and convenience store. Some tumbleweed rolled past the pumps, then the shadow trudged back into the store. Why were the lights suddenly doused in the store? he wondered. Was the shadow an MIB plant? Randall kept scouring the vast darkness of the desert, licking dry lips, wishing he could somehow control the runaway hammering of his heart before it blew like a grenade. By now they should have bypassed lockdown. By now he should be spotting the bright white beams of the helicopter searchlights. Or maybe they'd just roll up an armada of military vehicles, MIBs swarming the motel, kicking in doors. Anything was possible, given what he knew.

"There's no anthrax contamination, is there?"

He looked over his shoulder, let the drape fall over the window, covering up a sill littered with the fat bodies of dead flies. It was a dingy, grim room, but given the whole clapboard, ghost-town look of the motel, he hadn't arrived here expecting a hot tub, wet bar or wall-to-wall carpet. It was enough that they were still breathing.

If nothing else, he was grateful for her help, but he wanted her gone, for her own safety. She had paid for the room in cash, left a sufficient deposit for long-distance calls. She now sat on the edge of the twin bed, smoking a cigarette, the call to her Justice Department source already made. In the soft light cast from the lamp on the nightstand, Randall guessed her age somewhere in the mid- to late thirties. Brunette, hair tied back in a ponytail, blue eyes that looked at him, and the world at large, he suspected, more out of curiosity than fear. Her clothing was dark, camouflage for her little sneak-and-peek on the installation, he figured. She was nicely put together, holding up in the right places. He felt self-conscious of his portly body all of a sudden, the few wisps of white hair plastered now by dried sweat over a mostly bald head. For a moment, she made him long for his youth, and simpler times.

"It's something else, something far worse than anthrax."

"I hear the reporter coming out in you," he said.

"You're scared to death—that much is obvious," she replied, her gaze measuring, waiting for him to respond. "I've been out there, during the day, too. I've seen these crew-cut guys dressed in black, walking all over a desert supposedly crawling with anthrax spores. No masks with rebreathers, no decontamination suits, just some real spooky-looking guys in black with machine guns, guys that make G. Gordon Liddy look like some yuppie in comparison. The anthrax signs are just a ruse, another lie to cover up what's really going on inside that mountain. Am I right?''

He turned away from her probing stare. "I heard you on the phone. What's the story?"

She sighed, clearly frustrated with his evasive tactics. "If you were listening, then you know I'm waiting to be called back. I've put in the SOS. Naturally I didn't want to say too much over the phone, but my source got the general drift. I'll know something in the next ten minutes or so."

"You don't want to say anything more than necessary. You don't know these people. They can do anything. Even murd—"

"Murder? Were you going to say murder? Jonathan, who are they? We're talking about the United States government here, not some Third World dictatorship where a regime of thugs can slaughter their own people and never be held accountable. Talk to me, please. I want to help."

"I... If..."

He cursed himself for being walked into the start of some hardball Q and A by the woman. He had just opened the door, the gates to hell, in fact, and knew she wasn't about to let it go.

Damn his big mouth! It was the fear, plain and simple.

Randall moved for the dresser, picked up one of the two bottles of orange juice she'd purchased at the store. His mouth was parched, and he drank with all the greed of a dying man. The juice went down sweet. Strange, he thought, how the simple things in life took on such stature when you never knew if this moment would be your last. He wondered if this was how a condemned man felt.

How did he tell her the truth? he wondered. How could he? Even he still couldn't believe it, but he'd seen things with his own eyes...

He shuddered as he recalled certain images, the kind of things he could only imagine the Nazis did.

"What are you, Jonathan? Nuclear physicist? An aerospace engineer?"

"My specialty is chemical and biological warfare."

A long silence, then she said, "That's it, that's all you're going to tell me?"

"For now. It's best that way."

"Look, I can lay all the facts in the world on you," she said, "about Utah, but I don't work for *National Geographic*. I can sit here and tell you how this is the second driest of the fifty states, how two-thirds of 54.4 million acres here is owned by Uncle Sam. You have military bases all over the desert out here, some classified, some not, the military still out here testing nukes underground despite all the treaties about testing bans. You've got Lockheed, McDonnell Douglas, Martin Marietta out here—Utah, Nevada, Arizona, New Mexico—building classified aircraft. I've heard all the rumors how they borrowed technology for stealth fighters from aliens who have been crash landing all over the Southwest since Roswell. I've even heard how all the radioactive fallout from nuclear testing since after World War II has mutated scorpions and tarantulas into predatory monsters the size of Dobermans. I've yet to see one of them, but I've hung around the saloons enough, and, well, I guess you get a few beers in one of these desert rats and they'll tell you anything."

"For a story."

"It's not just about the story."

"Money, maybe?"

"I have money."

"Fame, then. A round on the talk shows."

She scowled. "I'm not in search of my fifteen minutes."

"Right. You're looking for the truth. Lady, believe me when I tell you, this is not the *X-Files*. This is real, this is something so…"

"Say it."

He slammed the bottle on the dresser. "No."

"Why? If you told me, then you'd have to kill me?"

Randall chuckled bitterly. "They'd have to kill me, only that's exactly what they will do if they find me." He watched her smoke, wanting desperately to tell her something, anything if only to get her to back off. "Sally," he said, pinning her with an imploring look, "you are in serious danger if they find you with me. You have to leave. Now. I insist."

"The call."

"Okay, then after that. If you leave, I will give you something…a floppy disk I took from there. It's a copy I made of some research. I'll hold on to the other one until these Justice Department people get here."

She stared at him, fear showing in her eyes for the first time since she'd scooped him up. "You're serious, aren't you?"

"Never been more so in my life. I give you the copy, then you leave. Okay?"

She stabbed out her cigarette in the ashtray on the nightstand. "I have one condition if I do that."

"What?" he asked, impatiently, the woman showing grim resolve. There was no time to malinger, wait around. What the hell was her problem?

"If something does or doesn't happen to you, and I'm banking on the latter," she took her purse, pulled out a pen and card, "I write where I'll be staying when I leave here."

"That's dumb. If I'm found here, they'll tear this place up."

"No, listen to me. I put it inside the pillow case. Say you're right and something happens to you, I can at least touch base with my Justice source again."

"And you'll tell them about the pillow case."

"And where I can be found. I can play cloak-and-dagger with the best of them. Say you run into some problem when the Justice people pick you up or they need confirmation of your story. I understand where you're coming from, as far as the less I know the better. I'll do it your way, but give yourself some backup in the event something goes wrong."

It made sense, especially when he took into account how stubborn she was. No, he wouldn't get rid of her unless he went along with her one demand.

"Do it," he said.

She wrote on the card, then tucked it into the closest pillow case.

"No more questions," he told her, then went to the window, pulling back the drape. He heard her fire up another cigarette, his mind racing with dozens of fear-edged questions. How could this happen in America? Who would stop them? He paced. Watched the window. Drank juice. His mind churned for what seemed like an hour with all the horror of what he'd seen, aware of all the future wrongs that had to be stopped, knew he was indirectly responsible. God in Heaven, if they managed to launch...

The phone rang. He turned from the window, watched her closely as she picked up the receiver. He listened but it was a one-way conversation for the most part. She grunted several times, forced, of course, to risk giving the general location of the motel, the room number, then hung up.

"Well?"

"It will be several hours, maybe even after dawn."

"But they're sending a team of agents, right?" Randall wanted to know, insistent.

"Not exactly."

"Then what exactly?"

"They're sending someone. A special agent."

He wasn't sure he'd heard her right, but knew he had, then listened to his grim chuckle fill the room, a death knell if he ever heard one. "One man? They're sending out just one man?"

1

Mack Bolan was mildly curious but highly skeptical about his present assignment.

Fisting the wheel of the military Chevy Blazer–style M1009 CUCV utility vehicle, the man also known as the Executioner kept his eyes fixed on the lonely stretch of desert highway ahead. The sun was beginning to rise to the right of Bolan's four-wheel-drive rental, soft bands of reddish-golden rays now rolling across the Escalante Desert, a no-man's-wasteland of rock, scrub brush and low chains of saw-tooth hills. He was maybe thirty minutes out of the airport near Cedar City, having deplaned from the Gulfstream C-20 with his large nylon war bag and an intel package, such as it was, all the particulars for this outing, something he more or less considered a puzzle with no one having more than the first piece to put on the board. Roughly six hours ago, the military's version of the Learjet had been scrambled to Stony Man Farm, where the soldier had been standing down before the director of the Sensitive Operations Group, Hal Brognola, had apprised him of a possible situation. A lower-level Justice Department agent, a man Brognola both knew and respected, had called the big Fed in his office and was lucky enough to catch Bolan's friend as he was making his move to leave for his suburban haven. The agent informed Brognola a journalist friend of his had stumbled across what she believed was some type of top secret military base in Utah, and the journalist had allegedly scooped up a terrified CBW scientist who had fled the base in the middle of the night. Reasons were unknown for the man's escape, and the all-around picture was damn sketchy. But the journalist in question was apparently reliable, came to Brognola with an A-plus in the integrity column on the report card.

Brognola had simply told Bolan, "Check it out. Could be something, could be nothing."

Well, the soldier was in between missions, the Stony Man warriors of Able Team and Phoenix Force under deep cover in the trenches of their own respective forays, and Bolan never liked too much time on his hands anyway.

There was always grim work to be done at any given hour in a day of the life of the Executioner.

Terrorists, international crime cartels and other assorted thugs usually only slept if they could dream of new ways to feed their greed and savagery. Bolan normally slept simply as a means to recharge his batteries before heading back out to slay new dragons.

Only he couldn't see the monster yet on this excursion. Maybe it was there, or maybe it would prove a colossal waste of time.

Check it out.

Good enough for Bolan, when it came from Brognola.

The soldier slipped on his mirrored aviator shades, anticipating the onslaught of blazing, blinding sunshine, where everything out on the desert floor would soon appear to float in shimmering haze.

He stayed the course, headed northwest, having already perused the satellite pics, courtesy of the cyber wizards at the Farm. Those computer geniuses, led by Aaron "the Bear" Kurtzman, had pinned down the installation in question and marked off this motel with no name where Bolan was to round up a frightened scientist who specialized in germ and chemical warfare and was supposedly on the run from who only knew what.

Enter more of Bolan's suspicions and doubts.

There were any number of military bases, nuclear-testing sites, government installations in Utah and just over the border in neighboring Nevada. Some were classified, but most of them weren't. They did legitimate work out here in the desert wastes of the American West. For the most part, they built classified aircraft or they upgraded—and hopefully guarded—nuclear technology. All the stories of little gray men, UFO sightings, giant lizards and other crawling creatures mutated by radioactive fallout in the great American West were the trappings of fantasy, as far as Bolan was concerned. These flights of fancy were usually drummed up by some reporter in dire need of cash, looking for a sensational story to dump off on the tabloids to secure the quick fix.

Of course, there would always be Roswell, admittedly with its own suspicious shade between black and white, the rumored military cover-up of the alleged recovery of the bodies of the little gray men who had crashed to Earth to meet their untimely demise, only soon to find their remains under the knives of human autopsy.

Then there was that ominous Area 51 in Nevada, with its strange and unexplained light show at night, witnessed by small throngs of the curious and the thrill seeker, eyewitnesses shouting out loud to all and any who would listen about how they saw incredible vertical liftoffs of cigar-shaped objects the size of two football fields, or small balls of saucer-shaped light hitting the skies and vanishing at speeds no earthly aircraft could achieve.

New and improved and larger versions of the stealth F-117 fighter jet? Harriers or F-16s, perhaps, showing off some breakthrough nuclear or laser propulsion where afterburning turbofans used to be? A prototype and classified saucer created by the Air Force, defying gravity and all known laws of aerodynamics? No way, the sky watchers claimed, not without extraterrestrial help, or so the rumors went.

Bolan had heard these tales of strange happenings, the unexplained phenomena, and each and every new story grew more fantastic and spooky than the last. Supposedly there was even something called Hangar 13 in southern Arizona, some black project buried so deep in Air Force classified files there were rumored unaccounted-for civilian mishaps in the area, bodies found strangely and suddenly dehydrated in the desert when a convenience store with rows of bottled water was supposedly within shouting distance. Well, apparently not even the talk or cable education shows would touch Hangar 13, if the stories about a media gun-shy over this Air Force black project were to be believed.

Sure, Bolan knew there was the unexplained, the unaccountable, even the supernatural perhaps. But he lived in the real world, which was measured by split seconds when facing down an armed enemy.

In the killing fields of Bolan's War Everlasting, it all boiled down to just the facts. Which, in turn, came down to the quickest gun or the stronger of two opposing iron wills determining who would survive to fight another day.

Whether foe or friendly, this time out the Executioner didn't even have a scorecard with a key player's name penciled in. In fact, Bolan didn't even have a name for the scientist he was supposed to round up, just directions to the meet site and a motel room number. The SOS call from one Sally Simpson had been riddled with innuendo, underscored with all the shady need-to-know of two crime bosses on the phone discussing business and paranoid of unwelcome ears.

Whatever.

Bolan rolled down the window to a blast of cool air. At that hour, there was no one on the highway, no sign of humanity that he could detect anywhere. The surrounding emptiness of both the road and desert fed his mixed bag of curiosity and cynicism.

Aaron Kurtzman had already done some homework for Bolan, hacking into various key databases from the Pentagon to CIA headquarters in Langley, Virginia, from the Department of Energy to the Atomic Energy Commission. The base in question wasn't listed anywhere, not even a name for a military installation in the area stamped as classified. So what was it? If it even existed, what were they doing there?

Or was this scientist on the lam just some disgruntled employee? Maybe strapped with money problems, or a bone to pick with superiors? Perhaps he felt under-recognized, unappreciated and simply hungry for that fifteen minutes of fame?

So where did the scientist fit in? Ninety minutes, give or take, and Bolan would find out.

Whatever awaited him in Utah, the soldier was ready to tackle the worst-case situation. Starting from the bottom there was the Ka-bar commando knife, sheathed just above his ankle. The loose-fitting black windbreaker concealed his standard weapons, the Beretta 93-R in shoulder rigging, the mammoth .44 Magnum Desert Eagle stowed in hip holster. The locked metal bin in the cargo area was another matter altogether. Inside the bin the goodies ranged from combat harness and blacksuit to the aluminum brief-case with a satellite link, from a mixed bag of frag, incendiary, flash-stun and tear-gas grenades to the Ingram MAC-10 in special shoulder swivel rig to the HK-33 assault rifle. The HK-33 was fitted with a tele-scopic sight for long-range kills, the attached M-203 grenade launcher a send-off gift for Bolan by John "Cowboy" Kissinger, Stony Man's resident armorer extraordinaire. There were maps, canteens, tools, a first-aid kit and a ten-gallon gas tank already topped out in back.

Gadgets Schwarz had put his own personal touch to the war bin. If Bolan was forced to leave the ve-hicle for any long stretch, he could activate the small black box secured inside the bin by remote control. Curious and sticky fingers would receive a nice jolt of ten thousand volts, the owner of such fingers most likely requiring a change of underwear in a hurry before further attempts to crack the bin.

In any event, the soldier was game ready. But ready for what?

Bolan spotted the dust wall boiling above the chain of jagged hills to the south. Even before he saw it, he heard the familiar bleat of rotor blades. A hard search in his side and rear mirrors, finding only empty highway behind, and the soldier turned his sights back to the distant dust cloud.

The tapered shark-shaped chopper rose above the dust storm. Bolan glimpsed the radar-tracking pylon extended from the chopper's nose a moment before the pilot swung the bird around, dipped nose down, and began streaking a parallel course with Bolan's military SUV. Bolan watched the chopper.

The gunship was painted night-black, and he marked it down as some sort of cross between a Black Hawk and an Apache, noting the minigun in the turret, the rocket pods on its wings. A prototype warbird, he guessed, the likes of which he hadn't seen up until then.

Another mile of rolling down the highway, the warbird holding fast to his position, and Bolan felt the hair rise on the back of his neck.

They were watching him. Why? Who were they? Army? CIA? DIA? He strained his vision, believed he made out a shadow standing tall in the fuselage doorway.

Before he could peg the distinct shape of his watcher, the shark-bird peeled off, soaring on to disappear over the hills to the south.

Unless Bolan missed his guess, somebody was attempting an introduction.

"I DO BELIEVE we have a developing situation, gentlemen."

Mark Tidwell squeezed his six-foot, six-inch frame back into the cockpit doorway. With a grim smile, he stared past his pilot and copilot, searching the broken hills flanking the highway ahead, mentally plotting his next course of action. He needed confirmation of their mystery visitor, and a little harassment wouldn't hurt, either, to get the ball rolling. Part one of his next act was already in place, awaiting word.

"That was a military vehicle, sir," the black-helmeted pilot, Carson, said. "Built for rough back-country, light brown or tan camo to blend into these parts."

"I saw it."

"Tiger Two believes they picked it up coming out of Cedar City," copilot Thomas offered.

"Hang back to his side, stay well in front, gentlemen. I'm not looking to spook our new visitor to the land of Mormons and ancient vanished Indian tribes, at least not yet," the leader, Tidwell, ordered. "What you don't know is we already tracked a call from Gus Kamlin's shithole back to the District of Clowns. Specifically the Justice Department."

That caused them both to turn in their Kevlar-boron-reinforced armored seats.

"Our ALQ-IX heat sensor panel shows just one body aboard the Army SUV, sir," Carson said.

Tidwell grunted. "So you've said—twice. I'm well

versed with the wonders of modern technology on-board this puppy, gentlemen."

Thomas picked up the ball, his eyes lit with a sudden hunger Tidwell read loud and clear. "One man, sir. Sounds like the Justice Department thinks they're on a fool's errand, sending out just the one clownsuit."

"If it looks too strange, Sarge, it should be no sweat if the Fed leads us straight to the running boy like you implied he might."

"Not implied, mister, it's what I strongly suspect, and want him to do," replied Tidwell.

"Say the Fed heads back this way with the scientist, what I meant was we could make it quick and easy," Carson said, his tone rising to near fever pitch. "Kill the proverbial two birds, if you catch my drift, sir."

"I believe it's been caught, Carson. We take this ride to the end. Kamlin confirmed the scientist is there, but if he's called in some Justice Department flunky to pick him up, well, let's just say I need to feel the situation out a little more before I put in any call to the major for the bombs away."

"Yes, sir," Thomas said, frowning, no doubt unhappy over being ordered to keep his hands off the gunstick for the time being.

Tidwell appreciated their gung-ho attitude, understood their zeal to unleash some pent-up aggression, given the Army's latest top secret toy under their command and control, not to mention the nerves frayed by a brewing crisis.

And the XH-10 Tiger Shark was quite the killing package, Tidwell had to admit. The prototype gunship, built by McDonnell Douglas engineers working out of Area 51 in Nevada, the Tiger Shark combined the tank-killing firepower of the Apache AH-64 with the avionics, all the radar, tracking and search-and-rescue capabilities of the Black Hawk SOF MH-60, only upgraded and fine-tuned to new dimensions. Like Tidwell, his flyboys were Gulf vets, only they had flown plenty of Apache sorties during the war over there, done more than their fair share of blowing up and killing. Tidwell was also former Delta Force. Sniping off Iraqis behind the lines was his claim to fame. He preferred being on the ground, a .50-caliber rifle in hand, but he had his orders from Paxson.

They were all itchy for some action, and that was plenty good enough for Tidwell. But before they started winging Hellfire missiles around and shooting up the desert with the 30 mm chain gun, Tidwell knew he'd have to check in with Paxson. Tidwell was counting on the major being so jacked up to nip their present trouble in the bud, that he'd soon enough get to see the Tiger Shark in action for the first time.

Confident the task at hand would prove just another day on the firing range, he still found it incredible that with all the Tiger Shark's state-of-the-art wizardry, it took a foot patrol to pick up the tire tracks, two miles southeast of the compound, and steer them in the general direction of their runner. So much for high tech. Well, the answer to their present woes was all in the Tiger Shark's firepower anyway.

Smiling to himself, Tidwell stepped back into the belly of the flying beast. The new day would bring all problems into the light, and hopefully straight into the Tiger's gunsights. Last night's trouble was soon going to be just a bad memory. All he needed was a "go" from Paxson and he could cut his flying killers loose. He picked up his handheld to scramble the ground units already in the area.

Time to rattle a cage or two.

THE CRUISER CAME out of nowhere, shot up on his bumper, lights flashing, before Bolan could figure out just where and how the hell he'd missed it.

Not even twenty minutes after the black helicopter had been lost to his sight, and now the sheriff of Iron County was pulling him over. Coincidence? Right, Bolan thought. Maybe the man simply wanted to welcome him to Utah, wish him a pleasant stay, send him on his merry way, complete with tourist handbook for all the sights and scenery.

Maybe when they served cold Budweiser in hell, he thought.

The Executioner clocked his speed at 69 mph. The last sign he'd seen posted the speed limit at sixty-five. His mental radar for trouble was suddenly blipping strong warning signals in his head. He smelled corruption, a setup or a tie-in to the black helicopter.

The soldier tapped on the brakes, dropped his speed, swinging off to the dirt shoulder of the highway, Iron County's finest riding his tail the whole way in to the final stop.

The figure in white Stetson and brown uniform that emerged from the driver's side topped six feet, two-twenty, Bolan figured, with plenty of beef around the middle. As if to stress some grim importance to the moment, the sheriff hoisted up the holster fitted with revolver cartridges, ran a hand over the ivory-handled butt of a large handgun, which looked like a .44 Magnum Ruger Redhawk to Bolan.

By now the sun had cleared the mountain peaks to the east, the early-morning blaze promising to turn the desert floor into a furnace.

It didn't escape Bolan's observation that the sheriff hadn't bothered to pick up his mike to call in the license plate. Or maybe they did things a little differently in Utah. Bolan supposed he was about to get a taste of just how much the law diverted from standard operating procedure.

Bolan rolled down his window, turned his head and found the big lawman giving the cargo area and back seat a thorough scouring as he slowly walked up to the driver's door.

"Morning, sir."

Bolan couldn't read the expression, the tone, but he sensed he was being measured. "Morning," Bolan returned. The silence that followed, the subtle hardening of the sheriff's features pretty much told Bolan this was a check stop. "Is there a problem, Sheriff?"

"Are you in a hurry to get somewhere?"

Bolan played it cool. "Not especially. I must have missed the posted speed limit sign. I was speeding, right?"

"Let me see some ID."

Bolan felt the weight of his weapons as he watched the sheriff's head lower an inch or so, the eyes behind the sunglasses most likely scrutinizing the bulges beneath his windbreaker.

"You're packing, I see."

No surprise or panic in the voice, the sheriff not even reaching for his weapon. It was a matter-of-fact statement, tipping Bolan off that someone along the way had made him as a Justice Department agent. How? Who? Was it the someone he was supposed to pick up, creating some elaborate ruse, weaving a web for an ambush? For what purpose? Or maybe the people the scientist was running from had already been snatched and squeezed for information regarding the call to the Justice Department.

The soldier produced his phoney Virginia driver's license. "I'm with the Justice Department."

"Show me."

Bolan pulled out the fake credentials identifying him as Special Agent Michael Belasko. The sheriff made a show of giving both sets of doctored ID a long perusing, then handed them back to Bolan.

"Let me guess," the lawman said, "you got tired of Washington and figured Utah was as good a place as any for some R and R."

Bolan tried to put some friendly into his smile but he knew it didn't quite come off. He was cold as ice inside. "Something like that."

After again eyeballing the cargo area, the lawman grunted, hands on his hips. "Well, in that case, enjoy your vacation, Agent Belasko. Try and watch your speed. Some of the roads out here probably aren't the finely paved blacktops you're used to."

Bolan watched as the sheriff walked back to his cruiser. The soldier sensed the suspicion, believed he could feel the lawman controlling his urgency to report back to whoever had him in his pocket. He hopped into his cruiser, banged the door shut and hit the highway, revving his engine and blowing a spool of dust up the side of Bolan's SUV.

The Executioner waited until the cruiser shrank from sight, then eased out onto the highway. Given the way in which the sun was hitting the distant mountain ridge to the southeast, he couldn't be one hundred percent certain, but Bolan would have sworn another cloud of dust was blown up on the other side of the ridge by the black helicopter.

Whoever was pulling the sheriff's strings had just confirmed something to Bolan.

There was a lot more going on in this empty stretch of Utah than he knew about, and the soldier suspected it had everything to do with one CBW specialist on the run.

TIDWELL WAS PATTING the business end of the mounted M-60 machine gun, standing in the rotor wash of the open fuselage doorway, when the expected callback patched through. He took his handheld, and said, "What do you have, Sheriff?"

There was a moment's hesitation on the other end, then Waterson said, "I pulled him over, like you wanted."

"And?"

"One guy. Justice Department ID. From what I could tell, he's packing two pieces, but has this metal bin in the back. I don't know…"

Tidwell thought he heard anxiety in Waterson's voice. "You don't know what?"

"I can't put my finger on it…I don't know. This guy, Belasko's his name, I'm not sure."

Tidwell clenched his jaw, irritated by what he felt was this redneck's show of small stones. "What, Sheriff, are you not sure about?"

"Hey, I realize I'm not military like you heroes, but I know men. What I'm saying, this guy didn't strike me as your standard G-man issue. Something different about him. Cold, I guess, like he's seen things, done things better left to the imagination."

"You're right, Sheriff. You're not one of us."

"Hey, you wanted me to take a look at the guy, and I did it. You want my opinion, this guy smells like real bad news."

"You're paid to watch the turf, Sheriff, not sound off your fears. You've been watching too many Arnold Seagull movies, or whatever the hell his name is."

"Yeah, okay, tough guy, I read you, loud and crystal fucking clear there, Rambo. Us dumb-ass back-country desert rats don't know shit about the real world."

"Skip the wounded-ego routine. Go grab a few doughnuts or whatever, but don't let him see you again. I've got this covered. If I need you it will be for some cleanup. So break out the broom and dustpan. Over and out."

Tidwell shook his head, disgusted by the lack of nerve on the other end. The guy was paid to do a job, keep an eye on the locals who might feel the need to sink their ship with loose lips. Sheriff Waterson was onboard only to report in, take his orders, pick up his five grand a month cash salary from Paxson. Tidwell didn't need the embellishment, the guy's anal-retentive view on who was tough and who wasn't. One Justice Department clownsuit en route, more than likely to scoop up the scientist, and the sheriff was seeing bogeymen. Tidwell chuckled. Something told him he was soon going to show Iron County's finest what kicking ass was all about.

2

The phone rang for the third time in the past hour. And for the third time, Jonathan Randall felt his heart lurch so bad he was sure it was the big one. Again he couldn't get his legs to move. Rooted in the middle of the room, he stared at the phone as if it were one of those rattlesnakes he was so terrified of. Who could possibly be calling him? Maybe it was simply a wrong number. Who knew he was even there? Sally Simpson for one. Maybe it was the woman, checking in to see if he was still breathing. Or the desk clerk, who would tell him he needed to pay up for another day by eleven or move out. There was only one way to find out, of course, but he couldn't bring himself to pick up the phone.

He kept hearing voices outside. Every time a door opened and banged shut he jumped, gasped, shot a look toward the door. And where was this Belasko? It was already well after dawn, the sun burning like the wrath of the devil already. Six hours, more or less, he'd been told by the woman, and it was going on eight. Maybe there was no lone savior, he thought, maybe the woman had duped him.

Shadows moved beyond the drawn curtain. Voices

outside his window again, low and muffled, as if they were engaged in some conspiracy.

The phone rang on, more insistent, it seemed, the third time out.

Randall felt his knees trembling as he took what felt like a long walk to the phone, decision made. His hand was shaking badly, also, as he lifted the receiver. He licked his dry lips, opened his mouth. "Yes."

No answer on the other end. The dead silence made him want to scream, demand the individual identify himself.

"Hello?"

Click. Dial tone.

"Oh, God," he heard himself cry, slamming down the receiver. They knew where he was.

He practically ran to the window, lifted the drape back a few inches. Two men were talking near a pickup truck and the Harley. Blue jeans and long hair, scruffy desert rats, both of them. Sure didn't look like any bogeymen. But the MIBs were clever that way, could disguise themselves as any local yokel. He'd seen them when he'd taken a vacation in Camellion, even if they believed he couldn't pick them out on a bet. They bartended, even waited tables. They thought everybody was stupid, couldn't read into their grim silence, or if they spoke they had that tone of arrogance, always talking down, as if everyone were a peasant.

The smug bastards, always creating fear, making everyone look over their shoulders, flinch at shadows, any conversation at Camellion always restricted to the weather, sports, the kids back home, wherever home was. Rumors even of several government employees from other installations in Utah meeting sudden demise. Thirty-something men in prime health, collapsing from massive coronaries. Death from rattlesnake bites of civilians who would dare to ask anyone at Camellion about their work.

He missed Sally Simpson all of a sudden. Then a fresh wave of fear swept over him. What if she wasn't who she said she was? What if she had been sent to pick him up when he was running across the desert? And now she had one of the disks.

He wasn't sure why, but he went back to the bed. He delved into the pillow case, snatched out the card. On the back, he saw the penned-in directions to some place she was supposedly staying, somewhere up route 257, an X marking the spot. Close to Camellion, too damn close, he thought. Only the directions marked off what she wrote down as "dirt trail, three miles east of Camellion, gray house at far end."

He slipped the card into the pocket of his windbreaker. If this Justice Department guy they were sending didn't show soon, then Randall would find his way to the woman.

Alone for hours now, he wasn't only going stir crazy but he also felt ready to burst out of his skin from fear and paranoia.

He heard a vehicle pull up in front of his door. Running back for the window, he was pulling out the drape a couple of inches when he saw the vehicle, a military-type SUV, light brown for desert camouflage. There was one guy behind the wheel, now opening the door. Randall felt his heart pounding, the lurching in his chest again, his legs shaking as he watched the figure step out, close the door, slow and cool. He was a big guy, athletic build. Dark hair, maybe an olive complexion, could be Spanish, Arab, Italian or perhaps he was just a little tanned. It was hard to tell with the shades, the dark clothing and the sun. The big dark man was dressed in black, from windbreaker, sports shirt and pants, down to the soft-looking rubber-soled shoes of some type—combat boots, looked like. Black clothing? Boots? And Randall had seen enough shoulder-holstered guns at the installation to spot the familiar bulges for what they were. But why wouldn't the man be armed, if he was from the Justice Department? Randall saw the slight shift in the man's head, knew he'd been spotted taking a peek, and let the curtain fall back. The guy had moved like a big cat, sure of himself. Was it one of Paxson's men?

A knock on the door.

He considered running, but the only way out was past the big dark man. He caught himself, drew a deep breath. It had to be Belasko. If not…

Randall put his hand on the doorknob. He called out, "Are you Belasko?"

The voice on the other side answered, "I'm the one you've been waiting for."

"Okay, I'm going to open the door, but I'm leaving the chain on. I want to see ID, and it better have a photo of yourself on it. Any sudden moves, they'll hear me scream bloody murder clear into the next state."

"No problem like that on my side."

He then realized the absurdity of his demand for identification. Since they seemed sanctioned to do anything necessary to protect the project and their masters, he figured the military men could forge ID, maybe even create for themselves the highest level of Pentagon security clearances if they wanted. Just the same, it wouldn't hurt to see the man's ID, seemed like the only feasible course of action.

Randall creaked the door open a few inches, braced himself for the flimsy barrier to be kicked in his face. Without looking through the crack, he saw the thin ID wallet slip into view. He took it, gave the credentials, complete with photo of Special Agent Michael Belasko, a long, hard study.

"Listen," the disembodied voice on the other side said, enough of an edge to the voice to jar Randall from his dark perusing of the ID, "if you don't like what you see, I can go ahead and shove off now."

Having taken it this far, realizing there was nothing left but to keep on taking his chances, Randall slipped off the chain, opened the door and stepped back. He held out the ID wallet, which the big man took and dropped into a pocket on the inside of his windbreaker. The big man closed the door, but left on his dark aviator shades. If he was going to be shot, Randall knew it would be now. He studied the face, the cool attitude, trying to get a fix on the big guy. He didn't act like Paxson's men. No, Randall decided, there was something different about this one, a confidence that felt real, not contrived and meant to put the fear of God in a man just for the sake of fear.

"What's your name?"

"Randall. Jonathan. I have to ask you, did you see anything outside?"

"Such as?"

"Were you followed? Did you see any black helicopters or unmarked cars?"

The answer was too long in coming as the big man moved past him, checked the bathroom. Finally the big man said, "If you've got something they want bad enough, the answer is yes. We might have a problem getting out of here."

Randall felt his legs give out as he collapsed on the bed. He was dead.

They were both dead.

TOMMY REEMS WAS finally about to drift off to sleep when he caught the rapping on his door. It was a sound that could have been trying to reach him from Mars, considering the night he'd just put in.

Try as he wanted to, Reems couldn't quite bring himself to move, much less get up off the stained sheet of the twin bed. More knocking, louder this time, and his cotton mouth wanted to growl something Eastwood-like across the efficiency, his little slice of hell in North Hollywood. After a night of smoking crack, he felt like a petrified stone, knew any movement of mummified limbs would require Arnold-like strength. No life in the arms and legs that he could find, not even the first spark of anything resembling energy. Whoever it was, he cursed them out loud, wishing they would go away, let him sleep it off, allow him those blissful drug-induced dreams of happier days. Besides, he needed at least six solid hours of a dead man's sleep, what with the porn gig in Van Nuys at four that afternoon. Considering the rep that had grown like fungus over him lately, it could be his one last attempt to reclaim the glory days when it used to work, quick and easy as snapping his fingers.

His first thought, filtering somehow through the sludge in his brain, was that his two little party girls had scored, come back to return the favors. Fat chance, he decided, as he gave the glass stem on the dresser a longing and hungry eye, wishing he had stashed at least one piece to get him right. As soon as the rock and his cash had run out, the girls had run so fast, no doubt straight for the next port of call.

Ungrateful little trollops, but he should have known better.

Hell, he had shelled out pretty much the last of his four hundred bucks on them, maybe all of twenty-five dollars left in his account now. What a sorry waste of time, trouble and money. What had they told him in rehab and AA about insanity? Something about repeating the same act, over and over, and expecting different results. Whatever. Just a bunch of pathetic losers with no purpose and meaning in their shabby little lives, sitting around whining how they were simply grateful they'd made it through another day without using. Not Tommy Reems. He had a life to live, big dreams, a major talent just waiting for someone to discover. Tommy Reems was going to be somebody someday.

The knocking again, but this time urgent, demanding. He swung his legs off the bed, then froze, wondering if there were any warrants out on his head. No, he'd already squared that third DUI with the courts. He had paid his debt—six months of it, to be exact— to society last year for the possession charge. The apartment manager had already nailed the eviction notice to his door only yesterday, and by law he had thirty days to clear out. Did he owe anybody else money?

His life sucked, no way around it. But was it his fault he was thirty-three, going nowhere, broke and soon to be homeless?

When he heard the knocking again, he snarled, "All right already, I'm coming!"

He found sweatpants, struggled to put one leg after the other down inside. That Herculean chore down, he weaved his way to the door. When he looked through the peephole, he thought he was hallucinating at first. In the narrowed scope of glass, he saw a big guy, wide as the doorway, dressed in black, the buzz cut and mirrored aviator shades making Reems wonder if he did, in fact, owe somebody money and now they'd sent some bone crusher to have a little chat.

"Who the hell are you?"

"Maybe a friend."

"I don't have any fucking friends! What do you want?"

"To talk, that's all, Tommy."

The friendly act didn't wash, something feeling real weird.

"Get the hell outta here, I'm not in the mood for bullshit games."

"I have come to make you an offer."

Nobody talked like that, not even in L.A. "Yeah, like the offer I can't refuse?"

"If you let me in, Tommy, you can decide for yourself if you wish to refuse it. It involves a sum of money if you accept. Cash."

He was too strung out to think, stand there and ask

a bunch of questions. The big man had him curious, especially the part about cash. He opened the door, found the man in black towered over him by a full head, and Reems was six feet tall. There was an odd smile on the man's lips, Reems noted suspiciously. He walked in as if he owned the building, looking around, something like a sneer coming to his mouth.

Reems peeked out into the hall, still unsure about cops, bondsmen, leg breakers. Nothing in both directions. He shut the door.

"Nice place, Tommy."

Reems stared at him, then chuckled. "Now that we've established you're a smart-ass, you want to tell me about this offer of yours?" Reems said, sweeping past the man, moving to rifle through the assorted trash on the dresser, thanking God he discovered the party girls had somehow overlooked taking his last cigarette.

The man stopped in the middle of the room, folded his hands behind his back. "You know, I hate L.A., what with the traffic, the smog, its shallow transparency, you know, the surfer boys and the armies of wanna-bes, all seeing themselves as the next marquee name in lights."

"Hey!" Reems barked, finally lighting his smoke with the fourth attempt to strike a match. "Cut the shit! If I want judgment day, I can turn on Falwell or Pat Robertson."

"If only you could, but you pawned your television last week. The air conditioner, too. By the way, you have exactly thirty-eight dollars and eighty-five cents in your bank account."

"How the hell do you…? Forget it. Tell me what you want and make it quick."

"Very good. I'll try and make this short and simple. Let me ask you first, is your life all you want it to be?"

"You see Bel Air or Beverly Hills here, pal? You see Pamela Anderson in my bed?"

The big man paused, nodding as if he understood something reserved only for the gods of neon and lights. Reems was growing irritated to the point of demanding the guy leave, when the man reached into his pocket and produced a wad of hundred-dollar bills fat enough to gag the entire executive clout in an MGM boardroom. He snapped off twenty of them and shoved the rest into his pants pocket.

"There's two thousand now, Tommy. Two days' work. When you're done, there's another two thousand waiting for you."

"Who are you? An agent? Did Skee—"

"Something like that," he interrupted. "And, no, this Buddy Skeebo who parades you in all your glory—which I hear is not so glorious these days—didn't send me."

Reems wanted to lash out at the guy's dig at his manhood, but there was four grand to consider, right there in full beauty, visions of a week-long rock party and mean hummers and endless supplies of Viagra dancing through his mind.

"Christmas could come early, Tommy. A white one. I could even find you a doctor to fill the scripts you need."

It was spooky, Reems thought, the guy standing there, no expression on that square mug, but acting as if he could read minds. Which, in fact, it appeared as if he could.

"What is it I have to do?"

"Well, it's a study-research group you will be involved with."

"I'm not much for socializing these days."

The man smiled. "Four grand, Tommy. I mean, come on, you want to sit around here and wish upon a star, smoke your life away?"

Sounded reasonable, Reems thought, but it also sounded too good to be true. Then he stared at the bills, held out right in front of his eyes. It might do him some good, get out of his hellhole for a couple of days, away from the laughing eyes, the whispers and snickers, the drugs. Clean his head up some, he might have a whole new outlook on the world, see his future a little more clearly.

"I'm sure Buddy can find a last-minute stand-in."

"What's life without a little adventure, I always say." Reems plucked the money out of the man's fist. "So, where are we going?"

"Utah."

THE EXECUTIONER COULD clearly see Randall was tweaked out of his skin from terror and paranoia. Before he found the CBW man's room, Bolan had spotted the three black vehicles, no plates, parked a quarter-mile west of the motel, but purposely left out revealing that piece of information. He didn't need Randall any more spooked than he was, at least not until he had some answers.

Randall was back at the window, head swiveling left and right.

"So, what do you have for me, Randall?"

Bolan caught the suspicious look as the man said, "Just like that?"

The soldier was growing weary of the paranoia game. "You have thirty seconds to fill in the blanks or I'm out of here and you're on your own. We'll start with something simple. How did you manage to escape?"

Still fisting the curtain, Randall said, "Funny you should ask, the woman didn't even ask me that."

"I'm practical that way."

"I clobbered the guard, one right across the jaw with a wrench, I lifted it from the workshop where they house those giant high-tech tunnel-boring machines. I don't even know if I killed him…God, I hope not. Violence isn't my way, I'm a scientist not a soldier."

"You just walked out of there?"

"Pretty much. I have my own top-level security clearance—the package included one of those magnetic swipe cards. When my mind was made up to run, I hacked into their security file earlier in the day."

Bolan heard about lockdown, how the code box would have to be dismantled, the search for the right wires to connect to bypass lockdown enabling Randall to make his run across the desert, gain time and distance. He heard about the woman, the anthrax sign warning of contamination, only it wasn't anthrax they were creating. He listened to the scientist spill his terror about the men in black. Randall did everything in his power to keep dancing around the truth.

"Slow down," Bolan said. "Let's start over. What

exactly is going on at this installation? And who are they?''

"They're ex-military," Randall said. "Mostly former Delta commandos to be exact. Roger Paxson, used to be a major in Delta, some sort of classified black ops. He runs the horror show out there."

"Which is what?"

"You know that treaty signed in '72, when the Russians were still our worst fear?"

"The one banning the development, production and stockpiling of biological weapons."

"Yeah, that one. You might as well wipe yourself with it. Supposedly, or so they tell the American public, these days we're only conducting counter or defensive biological warfare studies. Maybe you've heard the rumors how the CIA created AIDS as part of some planned population control. How the CIA was dropping mind-altering drugs into people's cocktails, just to watch their reactions. How the U.S. Public Health Service duped blacks with syphilis into believing they were being treated, but they were only gauging the full range of effects, the afflicted nothing more than guinea pigs, for God's sake. The Army was caught red-handed in the eighties doing open-air testing on the populations of San Francisco, New York, Washington, claiming what they sprayed was nontoxic and nonvirulent. You had dozens of mysterious illnesses break out in those cities, and more than a few dead."

Randall went back to desert watching, and Bolan asked, "You're telling me ex-Delta Force men are standing guard while some new form of biological-warfare is being created?"

"To sum it up like that, yes. And what they're on the verge of creating— Oh, God, they're here! Two, no, three carloads of them, they just pulled up!"

Hand draping over his Beretta, Bolan watched as Randall flew back from the window. The soldier heard car doors open and shut.

"You were followed!" Randall nearly screamed, as if accusing Bolan of setting him up.

"Settle down," Bolan warned, moving for the door. "Stay put, I'll handle it."

"You don't know these people. You don't know what I've seen! They're going to kill me. They'll gun us both down right here and just stuff us in some hole in the desert."

Bolan stopped short of the door when he heard the knocking. He looked back over his shoulder, watched as Randall paced, fidgeting with his hands. The soldier believed the danger was real. Or it was all in Randall's mind.

Bolan figured he would know either way in a few short seconds.

He opened the door, found a military-looking figure dressed in black standing on the other side. A quick search beyond the man and Bolan counted ten more near carbon copies with buzz cuts, black outfits, dark sunglasses. Same grim expressions across the board, only two of the men by the nearest unmarked vehicle held Colt Commando assault rifles at port arms.

Bolan looked at the man, inches from his face. "Yeah?"

"Randall's no longer your concern. We'll take him off your hands now."

"No."

"What was that?"

"Which part of 'no' didn't you understand?"

One side of the man's mouth lifted, the hint of a sneer. "Get the fuck out of my way."

"Before we go any further with this dance, I think you should know something."

"What's that?"

"I failed Anger Management."

The man chuckled, looked back at his comrades. "The Justice Department really did send out the clowns."

Bolan braced himself, knew it was coming as he caught the subtle tensing of the man's shoulders a heartbeat before the fist shot out, aimed to break his nose. With his counterattack already mentally mapped out, the Executioner slipped under the flesh-and-bone hammer, then spiked a knee into the man's gut. The guy doubled up, losing his shades in the process. The small army was digging into jackets, hauling out pistols, the assault rifles swinging down when Bolan dug his fingers into the man's windpipe and squeezed.

3

This was a defining moment, Bolan supposed, where the truth might begin to reveal itself. If nothing else, the show of force proved there was indeed something going on to back up Randall's fear.

The hardman had his shield up and was gagging in Bolan's face. Bolan's fingers locked with a viselike hold on the man's throat, arm extended and holding him away. "Get those guns off me," the soldier growled at the men in black, before reaching inside his prisoner's jacket and pulling out a Beretta 92-F, the safety off. The Executioner backed the MIB up a few steps and raked the seized Beretta over the group of men. They were cool about it, Bolan saw, not even a hint of anxiety or rankled confidence, not the first twitch of nerves to ruffle their strange, collarless nylon jackets. More than likely there was backup in the vicinity, if he read their arrogance anywhere close to accurate. Still, no black helicopter was about to throw him off his stand here. Whatever the game, Bolan could tell it was just warming up, no play left but to stoke the fire.

When pistols and assault rifles were finally lowered, Bolan called out, "Randall, get out here."

"Is this where we're supposed to tell you you're making a big mistake?" one of the men asked.

"This is where I'm telling you we're leaving."

"So, go ahead. Leave," the man said.

Bolan didn't find Randall over his shoulder. He was beginning to wonder if the CBW man had slipped out the back through the bathroom window.

"Randall?"

In the corner of his eye, Bolan saw the scientist venturing with tentative steps through the doorway. "Get in my truck, but stay behind me," Bolan directed.

Walking to the vehicle parked outside the door, Bolan moved his shield around the passenger side of his SUV, covering Randall as best he could from any sudden gunfire.

"Drop the guns! Now!" Bolan ordered.

Reluctantly they let the weapons slip from their hands. By now, Bolan had a small crowd of spectators watching from the safety of their respective doorways. His next move wasn't going to be easy, but he knew from there on he was public enemy number one as far as Paxson's men were concerned. And the more Bolan read their stony expressions, the more he suspected Randall had something sinister to deliver. Factor in the black warbird, his brief but bizarre encounter with the Iron County sheriff, and Bolan knew he was in this game to the finish line.

"All of you," Bolan ordered, "facedown." More hesitation, and he barked, "Do it!"

"Do as he says," the leader said, his voice cracking from the strain on his vocal cords.

When they were stretched out on their bellies, Bolan released his stranglehold on the leader and stepped back. After making a croaking noise and massaging his throat, the MIB snarled and took a step forward, obviously not ready to let it go after being shamed in front of his men. Bolan shuffled into the man's charge, speared out a straight kick. Slamming the leader in the chest, the Executioner sent the man flying back, arms windmilling as the gunner rolled up on the hood of the car. The .44 Magnum Desert Eagle filled Bolan's other hand in the next second, and he went to work, not missing a heartbeat as he began covering their immediate evacuation.

The first shot from the Beretta caused a couple of gunman to flinch and look up. Bolan strayed from the outstretched opposition, kept on blasting holes in tires, the mammoth Desert Eagle ready if one of them wanted to play hero. The sound of air hissing from deflating tread, the steady cracking of the Beretta shattered the peaceful early-morning silence. Quickly the soldier burned out the Beretta's clip, punching holes through all twelve tires, an extra shot here or there for good measure. Flipping the piece away, he drew his own Beretta. A slow walk back toward his SUV, and Bolan triggered the Desert Eagle. He drilled .44 Magnum slugs through the grilles, opening up radiators to hissing clouds of steam. Just to heap on a little more misery if they somehow salvaged one of the vehicles, Bolan triggered six more blasts from the hand cannon, two hollowpoints each to blow in three windshields, depositing enough shards and slivers on the front seats to keep them busy a while longer. Overkill, to be sure, but Bolan suspected all hell was about to break loose when he hit the open road. The warning in his head told him the opposition would soon attempt to return the favor.

Bolan backpedaled for the driver's side of his SUV, ignoring the watching eyes from the motel. He dropped behind the wheel, fired up the engine and peeled out in reverse.

"He's right, you know," Randall said. "We won't get two miles down the road before they call out the helicopters."

Bolan put it in Drive. He gunned the engine, gathering speed, blowing up a wall of dust in his wake. In his side glass he found the men starting to stand, a few of them slapping dust off their coats.

"I've taken you this far. Show a little faith," Bolan told the CBW man, aiming the SUV for the dirt trail that would lead back to the highway.

The Executioner heard Randall groan, but there were more pressing concerns on Bolan's mind than one man's nerves. At any moment, he was ready for the Tiger Shark to make its appearance, knew the MIB would touch base and sound the alarm.

Dead ahead, the soldier found nothing but a vast wasteland opening up, waiting on his charge, quite possibly even looking to swallow them both alive and bury the truth, whatever it really was.

"DO IT, THEN, and you will not fail, soldier. I've already scrambled a ground force with some of the best snipers on the planet, as you may well know. If Plan A doesn't fly, fall back to the contingency plan we just discussed. The six men headed your way will be under your command, Tidwell. Report back when it's done. Over and out."

Angrily Paxson strode away from the radio console, clenching his fists so hard the knuckles popped. Silently he cursed the latest slap in his face. Somehow he stopped himself short of driving his fist through any number of surveillance monitors. A display of rage would only prove he wasn't in control of the situation. The damage was severe enough as it stood, and the last thing he wanted any of his people to see was raw emotion carrying him over the brink.

"You realize, Major, we're talking about an agent from the Justice Department. Open public highway, since it appears he's heading back for Cedar City, if I caught the gist of it right. A big desert, yes, but there's bound to be a vehicle or two out there when they make their move."

They were in the command center on level two, which also provided living quarters for the workforce. The steel door was closed, just in case one of the workers was wandering the hall. Although Paxson had passed on the standing order that no CBW specialist was to go anywhere outside the lab without an escort, any trust he'd shown before had gone out the steel door right behind Randall.

Paxson weighed what Hamilton said as he stared at the bank of security cameras that monitored every corner of all four levels. Then he focused on the men in decontamination suits in the lab on level four, thoughts wandering to their work, his sense of urgency turning into something like sparking electricity in his veins, now with all the new problems piling up on his plate. How much longer before he had what he wanted? Sure, he knew what they did was highly dangerous, specialized, nerve-racking work down there in the bowels of level four. But he needed the pace picked up if they were going to obtain the critical breakthrough, especially now, given the trouble he had out there on the desert. He decided he would have to start working them in twelve-hour shifts, cut in half, ten on, ten off, but at least they would be working around the clock. He no longer had the patience to hear on a daily basis about recombinant DNA. He didn't want to hear about splicing genes, how difficult and time-consuming and intricate were the cloning experiments of toxigenic genes from the various hemorrhagic diseases. There was E-coli, yellow fever, smallpox, anthrax toxins, tularemia, Lassa fever, just to name a few, down there in the mycotoxin labyrinth of level four. In the beginning he'd wanted Ebola Zaire. Keep it simple by breeding a living virus, then converting it for aerosol-spray delivery. But Ebola, the most deadly virus known to man, was too hot to handle, and not even his circle in the Pentagon would touch a project with Ebola stamped to it. Even still, they had come a long way in a short time, had already bred the supervirus—an accidental mutation that, in fact, resembled Ebola, at least as far as symptoms went. The scientist even had a few test canisters ready for open-air dispersal.

Godsbreath. The name alone fit perfectly into his own judgment day plan, he thought. Eradication of targeted segments of the American masses, control through terror, then blackmail, followed up by the ultimate power play, the likes of which the world had never seen.

But not yet, he seethed. There were still details to work out, key people to maneuver into place. Not to mention the inoculation he needed, if he was to walk, immune and in control of not only his destiny, but also the fate of the entire country, perhaps the world. They were close, or so they claimed, to producing a vaccine. Thus more waffling and argument from his CBW team, the scientists almost talking with condescension to him as they explained that developing a vaccine wasn't as easy as simply injecting a subject with the virus. This wasn't polio or measles.

No kidding. He'd seen them in the hermetically sealed chambers with his own eyes, puking black bile, bleeding out from every orifice, their screams muffled by the reinforced glass as their brains burned up with a fever that could reach as high as 120 degrees within a matter of hours.

And now two men were on the verge of perhaps revealing the truth here to the world, maybe even topple a secret government within the government. A CBW scientist and a Justice Department flunky held countless futures in their hands. Unbelievable.

One guy, if the reports were accurate, and he had no doubt they were, had dropped in to rain on the parade. His men were bona fide combat vets, killers each of them, none of them prone to embellishment or given to suffering from bad nerves. This Special Agent Belasko had already snatched up Randall, kicked some butt apparently, disabled the unmarked cars in the process with a Wild West show. The hand cannon he'd used wasn't Justice Department issue, and his kick-ass take-no-names approach didn't fit any G-man's style Paxson had ever seen. So, if he wasn't Justice, then who was he? CIA? Defense Intelligence Agency?

"I'm well aware of the risk factor, Hamilton. It's why I pay the sheriff. Any messes out there, I expect him to earn his money. You do know what is at stake here, don't you?" Paxson laid a fiery stare on Hamilton, who stood ramrod stiff by the radar screen.

"You mean the end game, sir?"

"Yes."

Hamilton nodded. "Indeed, I do, sir. I only..."

"You only what?"

"I only hope this little glitch doesn't somehow derail us from taking our rightful place."

"We will not fail, Hamilton. This country needs us—it wants us in the Oval Office. They don't know it yet, but a few good men are going to save the United States of America, even if a few million civilians have to be sacrificed in the process."

THE EXECUTIONER HAD the HK-33 assault rifle and small nylon satchel, stuffed with spare clips and a mix of grenades for the M-203, out of the war bin and in his hands as soon as he found the first empty stretch free of military men, black gunships or any other watching eyes.

The soldier hit the small button on the remote box, activating Schwarz's labor of love. Then Bolan searched the desert on both sides of the highway, combat senses on fire. They were out there somewhere; he could almost feel them, circling in, hungry to end the hunt.

The sun was already burning, high above the low hills and mesas, blazing like a furnace over the broken-up brown sea studded with scrub brush, juniper and cactus. With the shimmering haze rising off the desert floor, it was difficult, if not impossible, to spot any armed figure who might be lying in wait, even pinpoint a jeep or Humvee out there until it was rolling their way. There was a silence all around Bolan, a quiet stillness he trusted less the longer it lasted. He moved from the rear of the SUV, then stood beside the door, watching the sky, scouring the desert again. He found Randall constantly scanning the landscape.

''What's that?''

Bolan followed the CBW man's stare down the highway. A dark van materialized out of the heat mist. The soldier leaned sideways, the assault rifle barrel down against his leg, hidden from view of whoever was in the van. It was only the second vehicle they'd encountered since he'd put a quick five miles or so to what he hoped were still stranded military men. It was already pushing ninety degrees, Bolan figured, and he felt the first dribbles of sweat break from his forehead. He squinted behind his shades, forcing the sweat to trickle past his eyes. Maybe it was Randall contaminating him with a little paranoia, or not knowing what course of action the opposition would embark on, or all the unanswered questions, but Bolan was starting to feel his own nerves taken to the razor's edge.

Bolan held his ground, ready for anything. As the van blew past him at well over the posted speed limit, the soldier caught a glimpse of a man and woman behind the windshield. Turning his back on the van, he took a 40 mm fragmentation grenade from the satchel, loaded up the M-203's breech. The major threat on open highway would be the Tiger Shark. If the fuselage skin was designed anything like the

Apache, Bolan knew it was capable of absorbing 23 mm rounds and flying safely on. The stub pylons he'd seen earlier housed either Hellfire missiles or Hydra rockets, both of which were most likely laser guided and heat seeking. Anything at all like the Apache, and Bolan knew it could hold up in one piece from a vertical crash up to a little over forty feet.

If the Tiger Shark began the fireworks, the soldier believed his only course of action would be a full-bore run with the SUV into the hills, secure cover, take it to the enemy on foot. The one difference he'd noted between the Tiger Shark and the Apache was the cargo and troop hold behind the cockpit, an open doorway on the side leading into the bird. It could prove the one hole in the armor.

"Come on, come on, what are you waiting for, Belasko?"

The soldier hopped behind the wheel. "Buckle up, Randall, and try to keep it together."

The scientist buckled himself in, but not before he gave the assault-rifle-grenade-launcher combo a look with more stark fear in his eyes.

Bolan wedged the assault rifle in the space between the two front seats. "You got it, I'm expecting company." He pulled off the shoulder, quickly shot the rig up to sixty miles per hour and held it smooth and steady. "Can you tell me how many of those black choppers Paxson may have?"

"When I was brought in from Nevada I counted two, I think, at least the ones that looked armed. Two others were grounded—I saw radar and tracking antennae, but I didn't get that good a look. The choppers are the problem, aren't they? Yes, I can see it on your face. Believe me, Belasko, they will blow us off this highway, and just fly on. They'll deny everything, of course, cover up…''

"Settle down. Talk to me. Do you have some proof of what they're doing at this installation?"

Bolan glimpsed Randall patting his windbreaker on the left side of his chest. "A disk. It has detailed information on the work being done there. There are computer graphics of recombinant DNA, molecular breakdowns for gene splicing, my daily progress report."

"Of what?"

Randall heaved a breath. "Paxson calls it Godsbreath. It's a doomsday virus we mutated from several highly virulent hemorrhagic diseases."

Randall lapsed into grim silence, and Bolan said, "I don't see that you're too eager to part with that disk."

"Get me to Cedar City and on a plane and it's all yours. Besides," he said, then paused. "I left a copy of the disk with Sally Simpson. God, I hope nothing happens to her."

Bolan kept one eye on the road, but glanced from the rear and side mirrors to Randall. He saw the CBW man take a small business card from the windbreaker.

"She left this in case something happened to me. Take it. It's directions to where she's staying."

Bolan accepted the card, gave the detailed directions a quick but hard scrutiny, committing them to memory before he shoved the card in his pant pocket.

"I trust you, Belasko."

Bolan worked to keep the sarcasm out of his voice. "I'm glad we're past that hurdle."

"The woman, she risked her life to save me. She might be in terrible danger. If they know she has a copy of the disk, they'll find and kill her. Say I don't make it, is there a chance you could do something for her? Get her out of this state, put her in some kind of protection program?"

It was˜ refreshing to Bolan to find Randall concerned about someone else for a change. "Let's take this one mile at a time. But if it will calm you down, I'll see what I can do for the lady."

Randall nodded, fell into another long silence, then said, "You know, it's not hard to believe how something like this could happen. I mean, for starters, the Pentagon has a budget somewhere in the neighborhood of fifty billion dollars allotted them by Congress every year for so-called black projects."

"Is this where you start telling me the military has the bodies of little gray men stashed away in top secret desert hangars? Or that they've used reverse engineering on UFOs to create stealth fighters?"

The grim smile was the first sign of life Bolan had seen on Randall, other than fear and paranoia. "I've heard the stories, too. Whether or not they're true, who can say? I'm a scientist. I deal in facts, what I can see. Likewise, you strike me as the practical sort."

"What else can you tell me about Paxson and his project?"

Another sigh, and a faraway look settled into Randall's stare as he watched the desert. "I was contacted by one of his people—a cutout, I guess you'd call him—thirteen or fourteen months ago when I worked at Fort Detrick. I was doing legitimate biological-warfare defensive research. I'll spare you the sob story, the divorce, money problems, the twilight of what I thought would be a brilliant career, dreams of a Nobel Prize, all setting on not so golden years. The money I was offered was good, the best I'd ever seen. The few facts they told me about what I would be doing out here stoked the flames of my natural scientist's curiosity, I suppose. I took their money, figuring I owed myself one last shot. If what you really want to know is what Paxson intends to do with his supervirus, I couldn't tell you.''

''But you're thinking he's funded by someone in the Pentagon or Department of Defense.''

''Well, you can't just erect a classified military installation out here with a loan from the bank. One, by the way, that is authorized to use deadly force on civilians.''

''So, by the time you figured it all out, it was too late.''

''Belasko, I'm going to tell you what they're really doing there. You decide for yourself if it's something a legitimate democratic government would allow.'' Randall's expression turned even more dark, his Adam's apple bobbing as he swallowed. The man was searching, it seemed, for the courage to keep talking. ''Ever since we bred the supervirus, Paxson has been pushing us to develop a vaccine for Godsbreath. Think of Nazis and what they did to the Jews during World War II in the death camps. Think about how the Japanese advanced their own biological-warfare program during that war, using the Chinese, the Russians, anybody else they conquered and considered subhuman.''

Slowly, feeling as if some invisible fist were clenching his gut, Bolan turned his head and stared at Randall. "You're not telling me they're using live human subjects to test this Godsbreath, are you?"

Randall nodded. "More specifically using human test subjects to work out the flaws in the vaccine."

"And, so far, the sought-after magic potion is only killing unsuspecting guinea pigs."

Randall groaned, broke his eyes away from Bolan's hard expression. "You should see these...pathetic walks of humanity they bring to us. Drug addicts, the homeless, or just your average citizen fallen on hard times, maybe given up all hope, watching the great American dream falling into the hands of other people while their lives keep on crumbling. The gossip is Paxson's men comb through various law enforcement or other government agency files. They'll find and search out what they probably consider the dregs of society, expendables nobody would miss. No family or friends to speak of, no job, no future, no hope. Give them a cash advance, more money promised... Oh, God."

Bolan clenched his jaw, teeth grinding over this revelation.

"Before you judge me, Belasko, understand most of us worked under the threat of death. It was even in the contracts we signed with Paxson. Not so much in bold print, you understand, but it was easy enough to read between the intimidating lines."

"But you're telling me a few CBWs went along with the horror show."

Randall shrugged. "There was never a lot of complaining, at least not to Paxson's face."

"How many men you figure Paxson has on hand? Ballpark figure."

Randall shrugged. "Twenty-five, maybe thirty tops, from what I could tell."

"CBWs?"

"Twenty under contract. He keeps two specialists he brought in from I don't know where. They check our work."

"How many others on-site? Engineers, laborers, cooks maybe, like that."

"Hard to say, but I'd guess he has a labor force of twenty or so. Why?"

"Before I get you on a plane, I want the layout of this place."

"You're crazy if you're thinking you can just walk right in there and have a look for yourself."

"Determined, not crazy. You still have that swipe card, right?"

"Yes, but what if they erased my code?"

"I'll find another way in."

"Belasko…"

Bolan suddenly spotted the black shape he'd been waiting on. The XH-10 Tiger Shark swept down over the highway, a pluming cloud of dust blown up from the desert in its wake. The gunship seemed to fall straight from the sky as it hugged asphalt and streaked for Bolan's position. The grim set to Bolan's features, as he stared into the rearview mirror, abruptly silenced Randall, who swung around in his seat and cursed. The CBW man thrashed around, terrified.

The Executioner watched the warbird grow in his side glass, the gunship cutting the gap to a hundred yards, closing hard, nose down, the starboard wing lining up on the SUV. Bolan knew what was coming next. There was only one course of evasive action he could take—and it would require split-second timing.

"When I tell you, hold on."

"What the hell are you going to do, Belasko?"

"Just brace yourself," Bolan snarled, gaze flickering from the side mirror to the highway ahead.

The Executioner waited, the Tiger Shark soaring closer, twin walls of dust billowing behind on both sides of the gunship.

They were locked on, Bolan was sure of it, homing in on the engine heat...

Then Bolan saw the smoke and flame burst from the starboard wing. He heard Randall screaming at the top of his lungs, saw the missile blurring in the side mirror, a streaking metallic finger of doom, burning up the air behind at Mach speed as it zeroed in for the quick kill.

4

Sally Simpson finally gave up, at least for the time being, in her quest for the truth. She sat at her desk, stewing in frustration, as "Access denied" once again flashed on the screen of her laptop computer.

Thinking along the lines of UFOs and government cover-ups and conspiracies, or Area 51 and Roswell, for five hours solid she had typed in everything from "little gray men" to "lightshow," from "stealth" to "E.T.," from "Randall" to "J.R." to "anthrax."

"Screw it," she groused, the living room of her log-cabin-style house seeming to echo the angry edge in her voice. She snapped the disk out of its slot, shut down her laptop, pondering her next move. She imagined the computer was laughing at her, even the men in black she'd seen patrolling the perimeter of the mystery mountain base out there, right then indulging a good chuckle at her expense, scoffing at her feeble attempts to learn the truth.

And why not? she thought. They lived in some dark world, with their own arrogance over some sinister knowledge they kept to themselves. Nameless grim clones, laughing at all the ignorant civilians as they guarded the secrets to whatever existed beyond the gate, that sealed-off hole in the mountain.

It galled her not to know.

But maybe she was just a dreamer, she decided, a hack with only a few obscure credits on her track record, destined to fall through the cracks of a world that was racing past her with its supermachines and secrets. She was a straightforward, no-frills, salt-of-the-earth gal, after all, Smith and Corona as opposed to Apple and IBM chips. Well, she took pride, just the same, that she was born years before this supposed enlightened age of instant knowledge, the high-tech sorcery of the Bill Gates crowd, all that Y2K madness, the fax machine, voice mail rat race that consumed the time and energy of too many people out there these days, she thought. Machines, especially computers, had made folks, specifically the Generation X-ers and yuppies, lazy, plain and simple. Computers now controlled the world and could someday shape the destiny of mankind, even plunge the human race into anarchy if some mad hack found a way to plant the supervirus. Even kids these days, she thought, couldn't add two and two without a four-hundred-dollar calculator at their command. Twelve-year-olds were even Web connected, interfacing clear to China, with computers that would have cost her a year's worth of cash advances when she freelanced for the tabloids. She didn't understand. No, she didn't *want* to understand this evolution into modern society. Simple pleasures for the mind were dead, like reading a book. It was all in the visuals these days, if you can't see it *live,* why bother? When the written word was replaced by video stores and TV talk shows, where was it all headed?

She couldn't say. Nobody could, and that should

have stirred up the greatest fear since men dreaded Halley's Comet slamming to earth to bury the world in a new Ice Age.

Simple may be best in its purest, cleanest state, like day to night, she thought, but today simple truth and uncomplicated learning had gone the way of the dinosaur, made extinct by that Ice Age of high-tech.

The sad, sorry truth was that she was no computer whiz, no genius hacker who could break codes that would open the doors to hit her in the eyes with the blinding light of wisdom.

Randall. A tired, old man, was scared out of his mind about something. But what? Terrified of being hunted down like some animal, slaughtered on the spot. By whom? Why? Sure enough, there was something genuine, she recalled, to the CBW man's terror. The truth behind his fear and paranoia was on the disk. Of course, he hadn't parted with the password that would allow her to access whatever truth was being hidden at the top secret installation. It was enough that he had parted with his identity, revealed in a moment of vulnerability to her prodding his title as a CBW specialist.

She tucked the disk in the top drawer of her desk, slamming it out of frustration. Just her luck, the biggest story since Roswell, maybe, and she was denied.

It all fit somehow, she brooded, standing, lighting a cigarette. All her life she had been denied the brass ring, or so it seemed. Couldn't finish college and obtain that degree in journalism because her parents simply didn't have the money; the student loan was denied because the bank placed her folks in the realm of the financially untrustworthy. Then a bad marriage to a career Army officer who drank too much, drifted into beds outside their home, the whole ugly nine yards run out with his constant condescension to her attempts at writing. A hobby, he had always called it, suggesting with a sneer that she should get a real job and help out with the rent and bills. Philandering bastard. She felt a flash of bitter anger toward the ex, hoped his new bride fell into his bed with some tawdry past of sex and drugs—and herpes.

She stared at the blank screen of her laptop, then slid the drawer open and pulled out the disk for another longing gaze. She felt herself burning up with the sort of curiosity one might reserve if the secrets of the universe, life itself, were within reach.

Or was it like trying to grab a wisp of smoke?

She flipped the disk on the desktop, heaved an exasperated sigh, then looked around at the Spartanly furnished living room. She considered breaking open the bottle of Chablis, then told herself it was too early in the day to while away a few hours in a nice warm wine buzz. There was work to do, a story out there on the desert to tell, something terrible going on that the public had a right to know about. But where did she go from there? Troop back out to the hills, another furtive sneak-and-peek at the hole in the mountain? And hope for what? A confrontation with those commando types who were authorized to shoot trespassers on sight? No. Maybe she'd be taken prisoner, marched into the compound to be warned in no uncertain terms by whoever was in charge to make herself invisible? Seen anywhere near there again and she would be made to disappear? Or questioned about Randall?

And what about the CBW man? It was only a small comfort to know she had done all she could for Randall, and she wished now she hadn't caved so easily to depart his side. By now Randall should have been picked up by the special agent from the Justice Department, on his way back to D.C., the truth tucked away in his pocket. Quite possibly whatever was on the disk was destined for the eyes of men who might even be forced to strike a pact with the devil, if the government was involved in some classified black project here in Utah. And why send only one agent in the first place? Maybe her contact didn't take the threat seriously? Or maybe there was no story to tell.

Suddenly she felt the whole house shaking, as if a twister were blowing across the desert, ready to bowl down the house, suck it up into never-never land, something out of Oz. The back door to her porch was open, and she nearly choked on the grit and dust surging into the living room. Heart pounding, she was nearly lifted off her feet, propelled by the gust of wind toward the front door as the floor shuddered with the force of an earthquake. Beyond the throbbing of her heartbeat in her ears, she made out the sound for what it was.

Helicopter.

She stared out the window, the dust storm swirling out there, nearly cloaking her Jeep Cherokee in a wall of brownish-red grit that was common to this part of Utah. It was hovering, out of sight, but why?

The disk. Whoever the men in black really were, they had gotten to Randall before the Justice Department agent; she was sure of it. If his fears were found to be anywhere in the ballpark of grim reality, they had forced him to spill his guts about her, or torn the motel room apart, discovered the business card with directions to her little house on the desert.

The dust storm thinned, as she watched the helicopter swing out for the low hills that broke up the valley to the west. It was a winged beast, configured like a shark. She knew enough from her ex-husband about military hardware to recognize missiles, as well as some sort of machine gun.

A gunship, she knew, one that couldn't only blow her little house down but leave behind nothing but a pile of smoldering ash.

Simpson kept waiting for the helicopter to swing around, fly back and land in the rock-littered dust bowl that marked her front yard. Instead, the flying monster hung, suspended, over the jagged teeth of hills, as if the pilot was trying to decide something.

She pictured Randall's face of terror, a small army of men swarming her place in her mind's eye, automatic weapons jabbing at her. They knew something about her.

Then, as suddenly as it swept over her home, the chopper dipped its nose and vanished beyond the hills.

She stood in the dust and the eerie silence. Given what she'd seen last night, the terror and paranoia of one man, she was tuned in to one warning instinct.

Trouble was on the way.

THE HELLFIRE MISSILE appeared to fill Bolan's rearview mirror when he slammed on the brakes. A microsecond in timing split the difference between living and being spread all over the highway and desert in a million smoking pieces and unidentifiable body parts. The heat-seeking missile roared overhead, seemed to skim over the rooftop as Bolan gripped the shimmying wheel, which threatened to rip itself free of his grasp. The soldier held on for all he was worth as the SUV whipped and slashed back and forth, shoulder to shoulder on a squeal of rubber, its chassis shuddering. He heard Randall screaming as smoke and flames enveloped the rig. The CBW man's fingers dug into the dashboard. The chopper's own hard charge carried it past the SUV, its sleek frame shooting on, blasting into the Hellfire's trailing finger of smoke and fire, rotor wash spooling a new cocoon of dust around the vehicle.

In the span of two heartbeats, sudden death was averted, but Bolan knew the XH-10 Tiger Shark had only gotten a first taste.

Bolan watched the missile flame on ahead as he rode out the whiplashing stop, resisting the urge to reach over and backhand the wailing Randall into silence. A flash of an exhaust pipe and the gleaming of an 18-wheeler's cab rolling along the road ahead, told Bolan—given the flight path of the Hellfire—that the heat-hungry doomsday was locked on to the tractor trailer.

The driver never knew what hit him, and Bolan could only imagine that last instant of shock and horror in the victim's life when he saw the unidentified flying object streaking into view of his windshield. The missile slammed into the grille, the massive fireball all but obliterating the cab. Whatever cargo it was carrying was lost in the follow-up rolling wall of the thundering explosion.

Bolan watched the gunship peel off to the right, banking sharply from the raging lake of fire, the raining shards of debris.

"Now what?"

Bolan ignored the CBW man, revved the engine and cut the wheel hard left. If he couldn't beat the gunship to the nearby hills and mesas, find a suitable gully, arroyo, whatever, in which to secure cover, the next Hellfire launched their way wouldn't miss.

"Belasko?"

"Hold on, and do exactly what I tell you when I tell you," the Executioner said as he jounced the SUV through a deep rut, bounded up and out and put pedal to the metal.

"DAMN IT!"

Tidwell stormed into the cockpit, still cursing over the miss, which had now turned into a sea of flaming wreckage that could probably be seen from there to Salt Lake City. A mess like that was sure to be stumbled upon by someone driving the highway, soon enough. Civilian casualty, no less. Oh, well, Tidwell thought, shit happened. That's why they paid a sheriff to clean up their messes, throw up the red tape and strangle off the outrage and questions by any state trooper or desert rat in the vicinity. If that failed, there was always the men in black to pay some busybody a midnight call.

"He's moving across the desert, sir! I can lock on another Hellfire soon as we level out!"

"No!" Tidwell roared at Carson. "You've had your shot!"

"But, sir..."

"Swing around and fly back up on his left flank," Tidwell shouted. He was looking through the reinforced cockpit Plexiglas as his pilot brought the gunship around, then soared back across the highway. The SUV was nearly lost to his sight, but he pinpointed the wall of dust marking their target's run. They were heading for the hills with its maze of arroyos, gullies and God only knew what else.

"I'll let the sniper teams move in, gentlemen," Tidwell said.

Another search of the wasteland to the north and he made out the distant spool of dust blowing up along the edge of a mesa. The two sniper teams under his command had seen their problem and were already moving into the game. With any luck, Tidwell knew they could have this wrapped up, thirty minutes tops.

"He's attempting to secure cover," Tidwell said, as he noted the bitter disappointment of his flyboys. "We'll hug the ridges, flush him out. If our snipers don't nail him, I'll put that M-60 to good use. I hope nobody has a problem with that, gentlemen."

"No problem here, sir."

"Sir, it's your show."

That settled, Tidwell moved back and manned the belted, tripod-mounted M-60 machine gun, aviator shades in place to shield his eyes from rotor wash. The Justice agent had gotten lucky, hitting the brakes at the critical instant right before the Hellfire would have scored to finish the game. Even still, he considered the fact it took some degree of steely nerve and maybe a level of martial talent to have ridden it out, aware sudden death was boring down, very little he could do about it, except hope and pray. The agent and scientist had watched as the Hellfire skipped practically off their roof and blew up some truck driver who had the simple misfortune to be in the wrong place at the wrong time. Tidwell had to begrudge the Justice guy credit where it was due.

No matter, Tidwell thought, smiling into the wind. A little challenge would revive the killing juices, something he hadn't tasted in a long time. Yes, a little challenge out here would sharpen manhunting skills. It would all be over soon enough, either way, and Tidwell knew he and the boys would be drinking cold beer over a couple of dead bodies.

Case closed.

5

The range to target was somewhere in the neighborhood of two football fields. Sweeter still, he was looking at a downward trajectory, no wind in any direction that he could make out, and the SUV was shaving the distance to his sniping point with each dip and jounce over the broken desert floor.

"That's right, ladies, come to papa," the sniper said.

This was looking too damn easy. Where was the challenge? Compared to what he'd done in the desert of western Iraq during the Gulf War, Jim Frakis considered this sniping job just another day at the office.

Show up, clock in, no big deal.

At least as far as Frakis rated his own talent.

Things were obviously not shaping up according to plan for Tidwell and company, though, and Frakis had watched the black smoke clouds billow from the wreckage strewed all over the highway. Ever since he'd seen the road of death during that Iraqi retreat from Kuwait, Frakis had come to love and look forward to wholesale, indiscriminate destruction—even accidental mayhem, as was the case here—especially when there was fire and spilled blood involved. There was something mesmerizing about the dancing flames out there on the highway, nothing like some guy who believed he was safe and rolling on, and suddenly his whole world blows up in his face. Poor sap, whoever he was. At least he'd gone quickly. It could have been worse, maybe trapped in the cab, burning alive, shrieking for the end to take him and stop the pain.

Well, the flyboys had missed the SUV the first time out with a missile, the gunship now zipping back across the highway, but way behind their targets now as the SUV bulled into the gorge, all but lost to the warbird's sight and guns.

Frakis had work to do. So the lean figure in brown camos settled in, stretching out on his belly, scanning the gorge below through field glasses. The SUV made it halfway down the gorge before the driver parked the rig in the mouth of what might have been a cave, or simply a pocket carved out by nature's fury in the side of the gorge. Tidwell had already given him the green light, but Frakis had seen the trouble as he made the hard run in the Humvee across the mesa, anticipating their quarry going to ground. The sniper team had beat an intercept point to what was marked on the area as Devil's Claw.

Just about showtime, Frakis thought as he saw the driver hop out, unable next to make out the words as the big guy looked to be urging his reluctant CBW passenger to move. The big man, supposedly just some Justice-issue clownsuit, was hauling out an assault rifle, looked like an HK-33 to Frakis, but outfitted with scope, grenade launcher, the works. In the right hands, he knew that puppy could become a rabid pit bull in a hurry. One agent, though, didn't impress him as nearly enough manpower to tackle the long odds here, no matter how much skill he might have shown off at the firing range. Frakis shrugged off the unexpected display of hardware. What the hell, he figured, two seconds or two minutes later, the big man could have wielded a bazooka and it wouldn't matter. There was no place for them to run or hide. Their butts belonged to Frakis.

The ex-Delta sniper's weapon of choice was an M-14 rifle, now laid out within an easy reach, just as soon as he found the opening he needed to deliver the two fatal blows. The outdated M-14 was still a trusty sniper's rifle, even though it was being put out to pasture by the Army. He had a 20-round detachable box magazine locked in place, bolted with the first of the 7.62 mm NATO rounds chambered and ready to fly. The attached Leatherwood Redfield scope was ready at a moment's notice to be fine-tuned and sighted on the targets. He would have preferred one of the high-powered .50-caliber sniper rifles they'd used on the Iraqis, but there was nothing close to the big-game headhunting piece in the major's armory. Overseas, he briefly recalled those glory days when his squadron of Delta Force black ops had infiltrated deep into western Iraq on the final day of the ground war. A total of twenty-six SCUD missiles had been ready to fly, pointed at Israel, but Saddam Hussein's last grab at a tarnished brass ring had been thwarted when Delta snipers had ruptured missile fuel tanks and dropped the crews with head and chest shots from as far out as three thousand yards. General Schwarz-kopf was so tickled over the stunning success of Delta keeping Israel contained and from possibly bombing Baghdad back into the Stone Age with everything short of nukes, that he sent a personal letter of commendation to Delta.

If only the general could see him in action now.

Six hundred yards, give or take, two quick shots, and it was a wrap, nothing remotely as difficult as the Iraqi black mission. Oh, well, Frakis decided, he took his orders as they came down, cakewalk or not.

He gave the mesa to his left a quick look, but his teammates, Johnson and Hubbell, were already gone, finding their way down into the gorge, just in case. Frakis believed all he would need them to do at the end of their descent was confirm his kills.

No fuss, no muss, fellas.

Frakis saw the big guy at the back of the SUV digging inside for something. The gunship pulled back on its race to the gorge and began hovering along the ridge, moving in slowly, Tidwell crouched in the doorway behind the M-60. The idea was to spook their quarry, drive them back out into the open for either Frakis or the other shooters to nail them.

A moment later, Frakis discovered the glory was set to drop—right in his lap.

The sniper found the window of opportunity he'd been looking for, as the CBW guy clambered out the passenger door, then stood there, gaping all over the place, unsure. The big guy barked something at Randall that Frakis couldn't hear. Talk about a gift horse.

Delta's finest snapped up the M-14.

BOLAN SHOUTED at Randall to haul himself behind the SUV, grab some cover, but the man stood out in the open, as if the fear had finally swelled his limbs with concrete. The Executioner was just about to snap off the electric current to the war bin, pull out and hand over the compact Ingram to Randall when it went to hell.

The gunship was hurling up a wall of dust on the ridge above the soldier, rotor wash creating enough racket that Bolan never heard the shot that dropped Randall. One moment, the CBW man was standing on the far side of the SUV, glued to the floor of the gorge as if he couldn't believe any of this was happening, and the next instant a slick finger of blood was spurting from Randall's chest. Before the scientist had even dropped out of sight, Bolan confirmed the direction from which the shot had come. Less than two hundred yards out, to the northeast, he spotted the prone shape of the brown-camouflaged sniper up on the mesa, sunlight glinting for a moment off the weapon's scope. Where there was one, he figured there could be two or more shooters on the prowl, ready to nail him as soon as he made a move for Randall.

Bolan crouched at the back of the SUV, peered low around the corner, HK-33 gripped tightly in his fist, locked and loaded. Randall was twitching in a growing pool of crimson, and Bolan heard wheezing as the CBW man sucked air as if he couldn't get enough oxygen. The sniper had drilled Randall through a lung. Bolan cursed. Given the man's age, the heat, and the fact he could forget medical attention, Bolan knew Randall was finished.

Still, he had to try.

The Executioner checked the ridge, found the dust cloud boiling from up there, as the gunship hovered out of view.

Bolan squeezed the HK-33's trigger, directing a long line of autofire, above and beyond the gorge, spraying the sniper's position, hoping a few 5.56 mm rounds would give him some breathing room to get to Randall. Firing on, the Executioner broke cover, raced to the scientist. Glimpsing the sniper falling back as his covering spray blasted up stone fragments and puffs of dust, the soldier grabbed Randall by the shoulder and dragged him back to cover behind the SUV.

"Code…access…"

Bolan looked away from the blood bubbles flecking Randall's lips, the gunship holding its position just beyond the ridge line. Mentally the soldier contemplated his dire straits. The gunship, he figured, was hoping to jar his nerves with the noise and dust, get him running into the sniper's sights, or maybe a team of shooters was right then moving down into the gorge. Maybe the Tiger Shark wanted another crack at him if Bolan tried some desperate evasive maneuver to cut out of the gorge in the SUV, give him back their own previous slap in the face with another Hellfire missile.

"Access…'Gods…breath…'"

Bolan glanced at the ragged bullet hole over the left breast of Randall's windbreaker. Fearing the worst, he delved into the jacket and pulled out the disk—or what was left of it.

Randall rattled a death gurgle, and took to the grave the truth about Godsbreath. Bolan shot a quick angry look at the blood dribbling off the disk and felt his frustration level rise a few notches at the sight of the ragged hole drilled through the top corner of the floppy.

Sally Simpson leaped to mind, the woman with the backup disk in her possession, but Bolan knew his problems at the moment could well keep him from ever reaching her.

The Executioner looked up the jagged ruts and deep gullies, a tortuous maze that would lead him to the top and hopefully lend him ample cover to get into position and take on the Tiger Shark with his one and only hope of turning the tide.

"RANDALL'S HISTORY, sir."

"You're positive?"

"Absolutely. But I've lost sight of the G-man. He capped off a burst...well..."

"Drove you back to cover, is that what you're telling me?"

"He's quick—that much I'll grant him. I'm looking now, sir, and Johnson and Hubbell are headed your way."

Tidwell stared down at the far side of the narrow gorge. "Keep your eyes peeled, and the second you spot him, raise me. I have Fireteam B on the way in through the mouth of this hole with orders to disable the SUV and to sanitize any mess you leave for them. Our boy's on the move, I can feel him. He's pinched in, dead meat. I'm sure I don't have to tell you, but just the same, don't start winging bullets around when the prong moves in to seal it off on their end."

"Roger that, sir, no careless moves on this side."

"Never any doubt. Over and out."

Tidwell wrapped his hand around the M-60's grip,

slipped his finger around the trigger. Two hundred rounds were belted and ready to rip from the man-eater bolted down to the floorboard. Tidwell craved just one chance to tear up Mr. Justice, head to toe, leave nothing but a few bloody chunks.

"Give me some lift!" Tidwell bellowed through the open cockpit doorway. "Out and ahead over the gorge, gentlemen!"

Crouching on a knee behind the M-60, Tidwell braced himself as the gunship dipped a wing, swung out over the boulder-studded and trench-cut embankment leading down to the floor of the gorge. He searched the jagged fingers of interlacing arroyos and...

There! It was only a shadow, obscured by the hurricane of dust blown down the slope, but Tidwell didn't hesitate, cutting loose on the darting figure with the M-60. He was positive he'd waxed the agent—no man was that fast. The M-60 barked out a long stream of 7.62 mm NATO slugs in a blanket of lead that would have bowled an Army squad clear back down the gorge. No howl of pain, though, no flailing limbs and bloody rag doll flopping down the slope like he wanted to see. Where the hell was the guy?

Tidwell figured Frakis had the situation covered on his end, was about ready to raise the sniper for confirmation of a body, at least a sighting of the Justice agent climbing toward him when the tall figure seemed to grow straight out of the side of the mountain. His position told Tidwell the slick bastard had obviously slid back to a point somewhere just beyond the gunship's tail. Tidwell was swinging the machine gun around when he recognized the stubby barrel fixed beneath the assault rifle for what it was, then saw the smoke puffing out of the grenade launcher.

"Lift off! Lift off!"

His screaming might as well have fallen on deaf ears as he ducked the object flying straight for his head. Tidwell flung himself to the floorboard, covered his head, for all the good it would do. He heard his mind cursing Frakis for his negligence in not mentioning the bastard was armed with a grenade launcher.

IF THE FIRST HELLBOMB grabbed their undivided attention, Bolan knew round two would have them screaming for the sweet relief of instant death, maybe see them bailing from the gunship for their lives.

Only one way to find out, as far as Bolan was concerned. If they ran and dropped out of the gunship, he was ready and waiting with the HK-33. The M-60 doorgunner, whoever he was, had missed his one chance for the trophy, moments ago, unloading a long hellish barrage that sent Bolan to ground. Only the Executioner had used the doorgunner's long and wild fusillade to backtrack away from the flying lead, and stumble—as chance would have it—into a temporary and nearly perfect fire point on the gunship.

No sooner was the 40 mm fragmentation grenade sent streaking on target after the muffled pop of the M-203 launcher, and the Executioner fished out the premarked incendiary round. The M-203's breech was fed and the soldier was tracking on when the smoky thunderclap boiled through the chopper's open doorway.

There was still the sniper problem for Bolan to consider, but his fluke fire point was situated in a deep pocket, near the top of the ridge, and he was secure, all things being relative, in the knowledge that for the moment he was shielded from the mesa shooter by a slab of granite. Even if the sniper managed to skirt the mesa and somehow line him up for a shot, by then it would be too late for whoever was momentarily left breathing in the smoke and cordite storming around inside the gunship.

The main flyboy attempted to throw the chopper into a sharp bank, soar ahead, but it was too little too late by the time Bolan loosed the 40 mm incendiary charge. The angle for his line of fire allowed him to drop the white-phosphorus round past the fuselage doorway on a slicing trajectory that ended with detonation somewhere near the cockpit. There was a brilliant flash of white light, a second round of smoke belching out the belly of the Tiger Shark. Then, even beyond the deafening rotor wash, Bolan made out the hideous screams of men helpless to do anything but feel the flesh being eaten off their bones.

The gunship lifted higher, then started to swing back toward the gorge before it began spinning like some crazed dervish, leaving it to Bolan's imagination that the flight crew was no doubt flailing around, kicking throttles and collective sticks in some horrified attempt to get the hell out of there.

The gunship was just about to come angling down for Bolan's cover when it suddenly lurched ahead, bearing down for the ridgeline, well beyond his position.

A wail of pure agony reached Bolan's ears. A flaming scarecrow then tumbled through the doorway.

Doorgunner or flyboy, ex-Delta heroes or whatever, it made little difference to Bolan.

These guys had tried to blow him off the road and ended up instead cutting short the life of an unsuspecting, innocent truck driver.

Not to mention they'd taken their pound of flesh from Randall.

The Executioner rose and released a quick mercy burst from the HK-33, kicking the fiery thing off its feet as soon as it hit the ground rolling and tried to stand.

Out of nowhere, stone fragments began slashing the air above Bolan's head. He flinched, ducked, then darted up the rise for another, but lower shield of granite. On the uphill dash to his next cover, the soldier spotted two brown-camouflaged figures to his right. They were charging down the ridge, leapfrogging ahead in a classic SWAT rush, one shooter blasting away with his HK MP-5 subgun from cover, while the runner cut the gap, went to ground and fired to get his rear gunner up and moving.

Bolan saw the unmanned gunship lurching up again, going higher, maybe a sixty-foot climb, before it started swirling in a long spiral back for the ridge. Autofire then slashed the granite wall around the soldier's firepoint, the leadstorm whining off slices of rock, while the relentless snapping of bullets overheard warned Bolan they were confident they could close rapidly and finish it.

Bolan hugged the face of the stone wall, mentally tracked the descent of the XH-10 Tiger Shark in relation to the advancing shooters who had appeared to be making their charge as if the burning gunship were made of flimsy wood and not steel that could slice a man in half when it crashed and blew.

If the chopper would just keep veering and falling...

Before the thought had one last heartbeat to finish the wish in his mind, Bolan heard the titanic hammering up on the ridge, and hit the ground.

The world around him blew up.

6

They had been monitoring the local and state police radio frequencies in the command-and-control center when Paxson overheard the citizen calling in to report an 18-wheeler on fire, southeast of the town of Lund. Fortunately the civilian had alerted Sheriff Waterson, who was right then en route to secure the scene. Unfortunately Paxson didn't have any state police on his payroll, and if they made the scene ahead of Waterson, he knew a barrage of questions could fall on the sheriff's head. From there, Waterson could break under the scrutiny of state cops, figure he wasn't getting paid enough to look the other way, maybe steer the whole mess straight to Paxson's doorstep. If that happened, the major could already see a small army of FBI, Justice Department types and whatever else the long arm of the law might send to the compound, firing off relentless questions, starting with why one of his helicopters was taking out innocent civilians. The rest of it wasn't hard to imagine. What were they doing there in the compound? Was there something he was hiding? Maybe they should confirm the base's existence with someone at the Pentagon, Department of Defense, CIA. Didn't want to cooperate? Well, maybe they'd just sit around until they got some straight answers, and by the way, you're under arrest.

His worries didn't stop there. After two failed attempts to raise Tidwell, Paxson had contacted Rudley. The bad news kept rolling in.

First, a Hellfire missile had, indeed, missed its mark on the targets, instead blowing up the 18-wheeler in question, scattering wreckage and body parts all over a public highway, confirming to Paxson a small war was being waged on the desert. And Rudley had reported the gunship was going down, even as they spoke, this lone Justice agent dumping grenades into the fuselage, most likely from an M-203 grenade launcher fixed to his assault rifle. The gunship had blown, all right, the eruption heard over the handheld in his ear, boiling up into yet another fireball that would have the curious and concerned sounding the alarm to the law. It was a fiasco, to understate the matter.

Striding through the parting steel doors, Paxson made a beeline straight for the Humvee, Hamilton on his heels. A Beretta 92-F was snug in his shoulder holster, while the Colt Commando assault rifle slung around his shoulder was the main weapon he hoped to use on this Justice agent, end his problems before he was faced with a series of crises that could expose the compound. He should be out there anyway, he figured, leading his men from the trenches.

He reached the Humvee, opened the door and wished there was a quicker way to get to the hotspot, but all choppers were unavailable. Both surveillance choppers were grounded for repairs while the only other attack bird he had at his disposal was watching the home of the woman who had been seen with Randall. By the time they flew back, refueled and took to the air, he could already be on-site, kicking ass.

"Sir, if I may, I have serious reservations about you going out there. Let our people handle it."

"They are handling it—badly. Just get me a chopper out there ASAP."

"It will take you, what, ninety minutes to even get there."

"I'll drive fast."

"By the time you get there, it could be over. Or there may be a dozen state police on hand, combing through the wreckage."

"Just hold the fort down, Hamilton."

"Have you forgotten our business with Iranians? They're expecting to meet with you in Dallas tomorrow."

No, it hadn't slipped Paxson's mind. He had a load of precursor chemicals needed to produce sarin nerve gas.

"You do have a company back there that needs to be run. If our plan is to be carried off, we need to be in Washington in three days. I'm sure you haven't forgotten our meeting with the President."

Paxson processed all that had to be done in the coming days. Iranians. A pharmaceutical company that he had built from the ground up with a few business partners. The announcement he was going to make to the President that his researchers and scientists were on the verge of a major breakthrough in the treatment for AIDS, possibly even a cure. It was a ruse, of course, this startling revelation only meant to get him into the Oval Office with a canister of Godsbreath while teams of his people took up strategic strikepoints in and around the city.

"Worst-case scenario," Paxson told Hamilton, "we bail. Take what we have already, with or without a vaccine."

A dark look fell over Hamilton's face. "And if they call our bluff in Washington? Without a vaccine..."

"One thing at a time, Hamilton." Paxson settled into the Humvee, fired up the engine, took the wheel. "Anybody ever tell you you worry too much?"

THE TIGER SHARK WAS down, going off in a series of world-shattering explosions that forced Bolan to maintain cover, ride it out while the sky above seemed to turn into a curtain of roaring fire. Whether it was the fuel tank or ruptured Hellfire missiles touched off by the crash, Bolan couldn't be sure, as the whole ridgeline above kept lighting up and a galeforce blast of wreckage and dust blew overhead for long moments on one wave of thundering fireballs after another.

One chopper was out of the picture, but if Randall was right, there was one, possibly even three more choppers, armed, and maybe even flying in at the moment. The soldier didn't think he'd get another chance to strike the same blow on gunship reinforcements. Next time out they would batten down the hatches, maintain altitude that would keep them out of range of his M-203, and drop the works on him.

And the Executioner knew there was still armed opposition somewhere in the vicinity. He wasn't about to sit still while they moved in, his adversaries most likely fueled now by rage over the loss of their comrades, knowing they had to pick it up a few notches if they were going to end the hunt quickly, with no more casualties on their side.

Loading the M-203's breech with a 40 mm frag charge, Bolan headed down the slope. It was difficult to make out the sniper, with the wall of black smoke sweeping over the gorge, but he knew he had to be up there still, waiting for an opening, one shot to nail the deal.

Bolan was moving through another gully, skirting the jagged maze on a northwest angle, when he spotted one of the two shooters. The hardman's face was a bloody veil, as he limped ahead, his SMG held out, fanning back and forth, his stare fixed on the pocket that Bolan had vacated. Being mangled by flying wreckage became the last of his problems in the next instant. The Executioner milked a quick burst from his assault rifle, aiming high, shattering the hardman's skull in spray of blood and bone fragments.

A bullet whined off a boulder to Bolan's side, urging him to tackle the sniper problem. Parting a drifting pall of smoke, his nose filled with burning fuel and roasting flesh, the soldier glimpsed the sniper swinging his rifle around, drawing a bead.

Bolan triggered the M-203, watched the 40 mm grenade sail on. The sniper saw it coming, was up and running, but the soldier was already feeding the M-203 another frag bomb. The smoky thunderclap reached out for the sprinting figure, the sniper having cleared ground zero. Bolan tapped the M-203's trigger. Under any other circumstances, it was a waste of ammo, but Bolan didn't have time to burn, being stuck in a long standoff with a sniper who could keep him pinned while any rear guard moved in on his six.

Round two scored, the fireball erupting several feet in front of the sniper, who appeared to race straight into his own death before he was catapulted backward in a flailing of limbs.

Scanning the gorge and both its ridges, Bolan strained his senses to pick up any sign of more snipers.

He didn't trust the silence, knowing the roaring flames eating up the chopper's hull could mask any sign of approach.

The soldier was heading back down the gorge, veering for the SUV, when he spotted three more armed men in camouflage. They charged through the mouth of the gorge, the way in which they raked the slope with their SMGs telling Bolan they weren't sure of his position.

Dropping into a gully, Bolan watched as they closed on the SUV. A gunner toed Randall's body, then went and opened the trunk.

Bolan flicked the selector switch to single-shot mode. The hardmen began raking the SUV with long bursts of subgun fire, stem to stern, all four tires flattening out, windows blown in within seconds, a cloud of steam rising from beneath the engine hood as bullets found the radiator. So much for a quick ride out of there, but since he hadn't seen another chopper yet, Bolan figured the killing crew had driven in.

Autofire echoed down the gorge, pulling Bolan's thoughts away from commandeering a vehicle as he watched a sniper hop into the cargo area.

The Executioner sighted through the scope, adjusted the focus, brought a hardman's face into clear view just as the gunner howled, came flying out of the back of the SUV. The strange sight of one of their own flopping around on the ground froze them long enough for Bolan to go back to work. Squeezing the HK-33's trigger, Bolan wiped the puzzled look off the face in his scope with a 5.56 mm round between the eyes. Another gunman was running down the driver's side when Bolan pulled the trigger again, delivering a message of doom, the slug catching his target in the back of the skull and kicking him off his feet.

A third man was still twitching in the dirt behind the SUV when Bolan ended his distress with a head shot.

Eerie quiet dropped over the gorge. Searching for more hardmen, the soldier moved down the slope, rifle poised to cut loose if so much as a shadow flickered in his sight.

The SUV was history. Slowly Bolan moved through the gorge and looked from the sprawled bodies to the growing puddle of water and oil where the engine had been riddled with autofire.

The Executioner stood beside Randall's corpse. What had started out as a mission of questionable importance had just crossed over into a new dimension. There were traitors out there in the desert who were prepared to betray their country by launching germ warfare. In due time, Bolan would learn the why, where and when.

Major Paxson, he thought, could bet his life on it, in fact already had.

The soldier gave the gorge a long last search, but he sensed he was alone.

Bolan was about to go in search of a vehicle when he spotted a familiar cruiser in the distance. Taking cover near a cluster of boulders, Bolan watched as the Iron County sheriff hit the brakes, jumped out of his cruiser and stood on the highway, staring at the burning skeleton of the first casualty. If the man was dirty, belonged to Paxson, then Bolan guessed his mind was racing with ways to clean up this mess, quickly and quietly, without the state police getting into the act. A long shot, granted, but Bolan was fast being clued in that Paxson could pretty much do what he wanted, when he wanted. If there was someone in Washington backing the man's biological-warfare program, Bolan would flush him out eventually, hunt the guilty down for a final accounting.

PAXSON WAS WONDERING how much worse his situation could turn when he snapped a look into the side-view mirror and saw the cop car surging up on his bumper. For a moment, he wanted to believe they were looking to cut around him, race on for the same problem he was trying to reach. A quick check of the speedometer, and Paxson discovered he was pushing ninety.

"Shit," he muttered, taking his foot off the gas.

Two, then three sets of flashing lights showed up in the side glass. Three cruisers for one speeding ticket? He didn't think so. At that point, he could surmise the state police had been informed by some civic-minded type of the situation, complete with a burning 18-wheeler, sounding the alarm clear across the state, wondering out loud to the cops why strangers were blowing and shooting up the desert. And there Paxson sat, about to get grilled by state cops, who, despite the fact he was licensed to carry a concealed weapon, would raise eyebrows over the fully automatic Colt Commando. No plates, no ID, no paperwork on the vehicle would start the ball rolling, signal the cops they were looking at a problem. Throw in where he was headed, if they were aware of the battle between his own people and the Justice agent, and he believed they might manufacture any excuse to hold on to him for a while until they got some answers.

Paxson was already mentally laying out his own answers.

When he brought the Humvee to a stop, Paxson waited a moment while the trio of uniforms stepped out on the highway. A quick check of the road, and Paxson took small comfort in the fact he was completely alone with the Smokys. One of the cops moved toward the passenger-side bumper. The third held his turf by the last cruiser, hovering around the open door. Paxson didn't see a mike in his hand. Good. They had a mystery facing them, three cops thinking they could handle the situation without need of more backup.

Adrenaline cutting loose in his veins, Paxson watched the mirrored shades as the leader stepped past the rear of his Humvee. The second officer took up a position between the back end and the first cruiser. A glimpse of the bulk beneath their shirts, and Paxson could tell they were wearing flak vests. Head shots, he determined, about as quick and painless a way to go as they deserved. He had to get to the leader first, envisioning his opening move, replaying it, back and forth. Daring, speed and luck would have to carry him through. Killing cops had never fit into his scheme of things, but then again, he realized the clouds of death he would release over targeted metropolitan areas wouldn't distinguish between policeman or citizen. In the end, it would all be the same. Dead was dead.

Do it, Paxson told himself.

The major opened the door, held out his hands, put on an easy face, as if there must be some misunderstanding. The holstered Beretta changed their mood, but it was expected.

"Hold it right there," the leader growled, draping a hand over the butt of his semiautomatic pistol.

"I'm with the United States military, Officer," Paxson said, shuffling three steps forward, needing just two more feet. "I'm on official government business."

One more foot forward, the trooper warning, "Don't move again, sir!"

The lead cop cleared his holster, was bringing it to bear when Paxson charged him, shot his hand out. Fingers digging into the trooper's throat in a tiger-claw grip, Paxson grabbed the cop's gun hand with his free hand. What happened next was more luck than any amount of daring or skill, as Paxson thrust back the gun hand, the pistol cracking. In the corner of his eye, he saw the neat red hole blossom on the forehead of the second cop. Before his second victim folded at the knees and hit the highway in boneless sprawl, Paxson ripped out the lead trooper's throat, thinking about that steel wall that held him back from snatching up Randall, a barrier that had allowed enough time to bring the Justice Department running to the rescue.

"Let him go!"

Paxson wanted to ask the remaining trooper, "Let go of what?" since there was nothing but a lifeless sack of flesh in his grasp as he released the gun hand, flung the piece of bloody meat away. Not missing a beat, he fisted up the trooper's shirtfront, holding him limp but upright.

"Andy?"

The trooper sounded uncertain, checked his fire as Paxson shuffled his human shield forward.

"Andy? Drop him now, mister!"

Paxson palmed his Beretta, duck-walking the dead man closer to the trooper, who kept shouting for the corpse to be released. A peek around the lolling head, and Paxson found the trooper's face framed just around the edge of the driver's door. Paxson saw it coming, the slight adjustment of the trooper's weapon, and neatly sidestepped the shot that spanged off the asphalt by his left foot.

Paxson braved another bullet whining off the road. He had the distance and trooper's position locked in his mind. Whipping his Beretta around his shield, he drilled a slug through the lens of the trooper's sunglasses.

Letting the corpse go, Paxson searched the highway, grateful for the seemingly empty stretches ahead and behind.

He ran back for the Humvee, silently cursing the steady piling up of yet more trouble. Three dead troopers were a nightmare Paxson didn't even want to dwell on. Since they hadn't bothered to call in the stop, Paxson figured with any luck at all he could make it to the battle, take out the Justice agent himself, then begin a long drive back to the compound before the bodies were discovered.

Paxson floored the pedal, spewing a cloud of dust over the dead troopers.

"TIDWELL? RUDLEY? Anybody?"

Bolan felt his lips tighten in a grimace as the sheriff revealed himself as dirty. He waited a moment, crouched among the boulders as the sheriff breathed a curse at the sight of the dead men, the flaming ruins of the Tiger Shark on the ridge.

"No one but us, Sheriff."

The sheriff wheeled, hand falling over the butt of his revolver, but he froze at the sight of Bolan strolling toward him with the assault rifle aimed at his chest.

"You? You did this?"

"The gun. Left hand. Slowly."

Bolan watched the sheriff reluctantly lose the revolver, then said, "You drive."

"And where the hell you think you're going? You kidnapping me?"

"I just need a ride. As a general principle, I don't shoot cops, not even bad ones."

"Well, that's mighty considerate of you."

Bolan spotted the riot gun locked in beneath the dashboard. He decided to let it stay there for now, anxious to expedite his evacuation. He allowed a few moments, though, to retrieve what he needed from the war bin, put his large nylon military bag and briefcase with sat-link on the back seat.

"You got any idea who you might be fucking with, Belasko?"

"Maybe you can fill in some of the blanks on the way."

7

"Camellion?"

"I said near there," Bolan told the sheriff. "Just keep driving, I'll let you know where."

The sheriff grunted, said, "Around here we call that place Spookville."

"Seems there's a lot going on in your little slice of paradise, Sheriff. All of it bad."

The sheriff glanced at the Executioner. His eyes were hidden behind the shades, but Bolan read the scowl clear enough.

"This where the Q and A starts, friend?"

Bolan looked away from the sheriff, who maintained a smooth sixty miles per hour, nothing fast enough to draw a second look from a roving state cop, but not nearly fast enough to escape the firepower of another chopper. If another gunship bore down out of nowhere, the Executioner could pretty much surmise the sheriff didn't have what it took—nerves of steel under fire or split-second timing when facing a heat-seeking Hellfire missile.

Bolan searched the highway ahead. The heat mist was capable of veiling a car or big truck—maybe even a gunship if it hugged the highway or shot up over a rise or around a bend, too late to react until it was nearly right on top of them. For the time being, Bolan didn't see any vehicles in front or behind, no sign of any more predatory warbirds in the skies, either.

They wouldn't be alone for long.

Now there was the strong possibility of a state police problem finding its way to Bolan, maybe even troopers getting caught in the cross fire. Sooner or later, someone would stumble on to the carnage, either civilian or state police, and it didn't matter how desolate or little traveled was this stretch of road. A hassle with Utah troopers would certainly slow Bolan, especially with the wreckage left behind. The cops may not know who exactly they were looking for to tie to the slaughter, but Bolan figured that troopers would soon enough swarm the Utah highways and interstates. There would be roadblocks, helicopters, maybe even the FBI getting into the act. And if the cruiser was stopped? What would a trooper think then, finding one stranger riding beside the county sheriff with an assault rifle across his lap, barrel aimed in the direction of the lawman's ample midsection? Sure, there were the bogus but supremely counterfeit Justice Department credentials, and there was always Hal Brognola to bail him out of a tight squeeze by the law. But any run-in with the law beyond a corrupt sheriff would prove time-consuming, and there was no telling what lies Bolan's driver would hatch to wiggle out of his own predicament, even if a few troopers had sold their services to Paxson.

The soldier paused to ponder his next move, weighing in the human factor where an innocent life was concerned. Sally Simpson was definitely now placed in harm's way. Given the encounter at the motel, Bolan could envision the military men putting questions to anyone back at the nameless dive, in particular the desk clerk. It wouldn't take much effort to find the woman in this wide-open wasteland, where folks tended to get to know their neighbors. Forget the disk anyway, with its knowledge to the gates of viral hell—Bolan was already on the scent, geared up, and not about to walk away from Paxson and whatever the ex-Delta man's plans were for Godsbreath.

If Bolan read Randall's escape run correctly, Simpson just happened to be in the wrong place, wrong time. There was a definite show of guts on her part for even daring to involve herself in something she was clueless about, then hang in there, even make off with the truth, or part of it, on a floppy disk. That disk alone could spell her sudden and violent demise. The woman was a freelance journalist, had obviously found a way somehow to get near enough to the mountain installation, stake it out without getting rounded up by Paxson's men in the process. With her natural reporter's curiosity and hunger for truth, the soldier could well imagine the lady right then trying like hell to find the right access code to break into the file.

As far as Bolan was concerned, that disk held nothing more than a way to nail Paxson if his men went hunting for Simpson. All things considered, Bolan knew it was up for grabs. It could always go either way, yes, the soldier grimly aware of the risks to his own life. And it was never a question of selfish motives, nor any hunger on his part for money or glory.

Cut down to basics, it was about right and wrong, and it didn't get much simpler than that.

Not to mention, of course, the not so little matter of kill or be killed.

Apparently the sheriff couldn't take Bolan's cold silence any longer. "You know, those guys back there...I'm pretty sure they were all Delta Force."

"I already know that."

"Is that right? Well, what I just seen, the way you mowed them down or blew them up, you're not from the Justice Department."

"I'm from the Justice Department."

"But you're *not* Justice-issue."

Bolan ignored the lawman's probing. "What's your name, Sheriff?"

"Waterson."

"Okay, Sheriff Waterson, here it is. I'm going after Paxson. He's going down, and so is everybody else who walks the walk with him."

"And me?" Waterson wanted to know when Bolan lapsed into another grim silence.

"That depends."

"Hey, don't keep me in suspense. Spit it out, friend. I'm finished as a lawman in this county—is that the general idea?"

"You're finished as a lawman anywhere."

"You going to arrest me? For what? You've got proof of something? See me taking any envelopes in the middle of the night? Got my phones tapped, heard me talking with Paxson?"

"You're finished."

"Just like that, you're hanging me out there, no hope?"

"They got to him, Sheriff."

"Who?" Waterson rasped, his tone cut by an edge of resentment.

"Randall."

"The guy on the run? Shit, you sneaky bastard."

Bolan glimpsed the angry surprise, smelled the fear reeking off the sheriff's bulk. He was about to pursue a line of questioning about the compound when he spotted the squat brown shape racing out of the distant heat mist. Bolan felt his hands instinctively tighten around the assault rifle. He was braced for another violent surprise, had come to see in his short, violent stint in Utah that anything was possible where Paxson's men were involved.

As the sheriff drove toward the heat-shrouded vehicle, Bolan watched as the dark speck quickly grew into a Humvee. The vehicle was moving hard and fast, even for this empty stretch of road, the tires eating up asphalt at somewhere around eighty, maybe ninety miles per hour. Just before the Humvee blew past them in the opposite lane, Bolan caught a glimpse of a stony face framed in dark hair. Even though it happened so fast, the startled look on the Humvee's driver didn't escape Bolan. The soldier caught the sheriff's jaw drop a couple of inches.

"Friend of yours?" the Executioner asked.

"That was Paxson."

Turning his head, the soldier watched the Humvee as it kept up its speed, flying on down the highway. Should he go after Paxson, force a confrontation? It was a tough call. There were still choppers around somewhere, and Bolan could figure the next time he saw a gunship they'd drop the sky on him. It was too

risky to chase down Paxson on open highway when
the man could call in a chopper at a moment's notice.
And there was Sally Simpson to consider. Without
her phoning for help, Bolan would have never gotten
this far into uncovering the nightmare here in Utah.
Another hour or so may or may not matter in his hunt
for Paxson. The compound would still be there, and
Paxson would have no choice but to head back once
he discovered his crack troops out there on the desert
were eighty-sixed. Bolan felt he owed it to the woman
to make sure she stayed breathing.

"My gut tells me he's going to check on his people. I don't think he's going be too happy when he
sees what you did."

Bolan faced front. Without looking at the sheriff,
he said, "Could be just a taste of things to come."

PAXSON HEARD the question form in his mind, then
wondered out loud, "What the hell is going on?"

In the opposite lane, the sheriff's cruiser vanished
within moments, swallowed up by shimmering heat.
He'd managed only a glimpse at the passenger, but
there was something about the man's face, his de-
meanor—a stone-cold look about him—that wedged
a ball of ice in Paxson's belly. That wasn't any dep-
uty, he knew, and the way in which Waterson barely
looked his way, as if hoping he wouldn't be spotted,
was ridiculous of course.

It couldn't be, he thought. Was the stranger the
Justice agent? Was Waterson jumping ship? Or had
the sheriff's vehicle been commandeered, Waterson
kidnapped and forced to drive the Justice guy? To
where? The compound? The woman? If the woman

was where they were headed, Paxson would be informed as soon as they rolled up on her doorstep. It might be time to retire the sheriff permanently.

Paxson saw the distant clouds of black smoke, spiraling for the sky like some Indian war signal, sure to bring the curious running. He cursed, knowing now more than ever it was set to come unraveled.

Cutting the wheel and dropping his speed, Paxson veered across the highway, bounded onto the desert. Focused on the burning hull of the gunship on the ridge, he used it like some homing beacon to guide him to the gorge.

Even before he reached the mouth of the gorge, though, he knew he was too late. He scanned for the SUV, saw the blasted-out windows and the rising steam come up under the engine hood. The Justice man's vehicle. Grunting to himself, he was now positive that Sheriff Waterson hadn't just picked up some stranded motorist or hitchhiker.

No such luck.

The Justice agent had bagged a prisoner, one who could start shooting off at the mouth at any time to save himself. Of course, Waterson didn't really know what went on at the compound, but he could throw around enough rumor and innuendo to inflame the agent's curiosity. And now there had been a failed attempt on the agent's life. If what he was viewing now was any indication of the Fed's martial capability, his will to fight and win, then Paxson believed he had seriously misjudged the whole situation.

No, this wasn't the work of an average G-man. And now this guy had a head of steam, not only wanted answers, but was looking to kick serious ass.

Paxson barreled out the door. He walked to the first four bodies littering the ground around the SUV. One of them was Randall, and he gave silent thanks for small favors at the sightless staring eyes of the man who had started this nightmare. If only he could raise him from the dead and kill him again and again.

Crouching, Paxson picked up the disk. His sniper hadn't only dropped the CBW man but had unwittingly ruined the floppy, which was now turning into rubbery gel as it baked beneath the sun. Two disks, though, and something warned him Randall had handed off the other to the woman, just in case he didn't make it. It made sense, at least to him, and it was worth checking out.

He tossed the disk away, felt his disgust and anger building, swelling like a time bomb of rage in his gut. He was finished in Utah, no mistake. He had expected a quick and relatively clean kill, with two bodies buried in the desert, no one the wiser. Of course, he had anticipated the Justice Department sending out more agents to search for their man when he didn't report back. But without evidence of a body, any pertinent players or eyewitnesses having gone silent or made to disappear, he believed he could have built a smoke screen of deniability, flexed his authority and sent them packing back to D.C.

Could have, should have….

"Goddamn it!"

There was nothing more he could do here. There wasn't enough time to give these Delta heroes even an improper burial in this wasteland. No, it was time to bail, and suddenly Dallas was looking real good.

Fate had forced his hand. So be it. He would just

have to take the five containers of Godsbreath, with or without a vaccine. It was his show from there on, and he was more than willing to accept the risks, even die for what he believed in. All along he had played no small part in the plan, but he was pretty much a frontline soldier, taking his orders, putting the pieces into place, out there weaving the lies for the others.

The goal, yes, which was the creation of a police state where the country would fall under military rule, a few men of vision and sound judgment who would make America right again, get the country back on track and steered away from four decades of moral decay.

He understood their thinking, in fact, believed absolutely in the same principles—and fears—they did. America was a powder keg of racial and ethnic tensions for which there was no solution in sight. The country was a sea of crime and corruption, money the only god they were praying to out there these days. The direction in which even the world beyond America was headed, it all seemed to him and his partners that the planet was swept up in a mad scramble to grab up ever shrinking resources, whether it was food, land, mineral or metal. The rich grew richer, fisted the reins of power while using the government or the media to brainwash the masses. Sooner or later the American dream was bound to blow up, because the party always ended. Eventually his circle of friends believed the masses would take to the streets in armed revolt when the economy went belly up and there were gas and food shortages. It was going to happen—even if they had to make it happen.

But the country, he believed, would soon enough

thank them all for staving off anarchy, even if it meant millions of citizens would die an agonizing death.

At the moment, Paxson needed to get back to the compound, contact a few key people in his circle, nail down the final arrangements if he was going to step up the pace to meet their goal.

He couldn't help but give the slaughter one last, angry look. He had ridden out here, hoping he could turn the tide back in his favor. But what he saw told him whoever had done this wasn't about to stop until there were answers and exposure of the program, not to mention his head on a stake.

Hell, he hadn't even seen this kind of killing over in Iraq, at least not by the hands of only one man. Who the hell was this guy?

Paxson moved back toward the Humvee. Going back the same way was out of the question. A moment later, he was sure of it as he spotted the flashing lights of a cruiser. It was racing toward the wreckage on the highway, still several miles to the south.

Grabbing the wheel so hard his knuckles turned stark white, Paxson backed out of the gorge, then began what he knew would be a long and nerve-racking race across the desert. Another day or two was all he needed. He only hoped his time didn't run out before then.

BOLAN SILENTLY ECHOED the sheriff's curse. One look at the sprawled bodies, recalling the speed and who was at the wheel of the Humvee, and the soldier could venture a good guess as to what happened here.

"Slow it down," the Executioner ordered as they

closed on the three cruisers, lights still flashing as if in some sort of sick mockery of the dead. Bolan felt white-hot rage carve his belly. "Stop it here and get out."

They were dead; Bolan was sure of it, but he still had to confirm. He wasn't leaving a wounded lawman behind.

HK-33 in hand, Bolan waited until Waterson was out of the cruiser. Then the Executioner piled out the door, alternating his watch on the highway and the sheriff as he moved toward each of the three bodies, checking for a pulse. Mentally he tried to put together what had happened here, for all the good it would do. Three cruisers had pulled Paxson over, but why? Someone must have called in the desert battle, and they were on the way when maybe Paxson raised their suspicion with his race down the highway.

"Good God," Waterson said, "looks like he had his throat ripped out."

Bolan rose from his crouch by the last cruiser in line. Something changed in the sheriff's expression at the sight of three dead lawmen, but Bolan wasn't sure he could quite read the look.

"This is what waits on anybody that crosses Paxson?" the sheriff said.

"Take a good look, Sheriff, at the kind of man you've been taking money from."

Bolan thought Waterson was going to puke, as he shuddered, croaked, appeared to fight to stay on his feet.

"How did he...?"

"Paxson doesn't give a damn about anything or anybody, Sheriff, as long as he gets whatever it is he wants. I've seen the type too many times. There's only one way he'll be stopped."

8

The black helicopter was never far from her thoughts. Simpson feared at any moment the gunship would return to disgorge a dozen or so heavily armed men. They would kick down her door, swarm her living room, some army on a march of rape and pillage, thrusting weapons in her face, a crush of barbarian weight knocking her down, pinning her to the floor. They didn't need search warrants, didn't have to Mirandize her. Her house would be torn apart, the disk found soon enough, and off she would go with the MIBs, never to be seen or heard from again.

It could happen, she believed, if she read the folks around here even halfway right.

The three times she'd trooped to Camellion, either for a decent meal or to gather some idea what kind of work people were doing out here in Utah, she came away feeling as if she had just walked among the dead. No one smiled, everyone struggling to simply look each other in the eye, it seemed. Any conversation she had attempted to start with a resident of Camellion was one-sided, with her asking all the questions and getting either a grunt, a shake of the head or the straight brush-off, meaning they simply turned and walked away. No goodbye, kiss-off, nothing, not even the standard "no comment." Anywhere else in the world, she would have screamed in outrage at their rudeness, but in Camellion she quickly sensed it was something far worse than lack of manners.

People were scared. Of who or what, she couldn't say, but she could dare to speculate. At least to herself.

If only she knew what had happened to Randall. Had the Justice Department agent even picked him up? Knowing something, anything, might stop her pacing around the house, peeking past the drapes, searching the desert and the hills for bogeymen. An image of Randall acting in precisely the same paranoid manner halted her for all of two seconds. If she could see herself, Simpson thought, she would probably laugh at the sight, tweaked out on fear, turning the television on then off, rushing back and forth to the front window. What to do? Where to go? Whom to turn to? Each hour grinding down her frayed nerves even more. Unable to concentrate on the simplest task. Feeling as if she'd burst out of her skin.

She could always call the motel with no name, someplace that was actually referred to as Kamlin's in the phone directory, but there was the chance she'd been seen leaving Randall's room by a spying man in black. Or maybe the owner himself had been questioned, warned to alert the military men if anyone called for Randall. Could they tap into anyone's phone line at will? Could they hear conversations behind closed doors, every inch of this part of Utah bugged and wired up, with parabolic mikes on the black choppers, hovering over people's homes, listening to their dinner conversations or pillow talk? Could they kill innocent people and get away with it? Were they always watching those civilians they didn't trust or suspected of seeing too much out there in the desert, the MIBs always perusing a list of suspicious persons they kept on file, seeking them out to intimidate or worse?

She stared at the phone, considered calling her friend at the Justice Department. Even with some unforeseen delay—a car breaking down on the desert highway from maybe an overheated radiator, or the Justice agent even getting lost for a while before he found the motel—someone in Washington should know something by now, should have at least heard from the man they'd sent out.

Or maybe not. Perhaps the men in black had killed the Justice agent and Randall, left them for the buzzards and the coyotes, far out in the vast emptiness of a desert where no one but the foolhardy would ever dare go.

She heard a car pull up out front. She watched through the crack between the drape and window as a police cruiser parked near her porch. She had never been one to even think about owning, much less carrying a gun, but right then she wished she had something to defend herself with. And why would the cops show up at her house anyway?

She felt foolish for a moment, running to the window, going through all the exact same drape-hugging peek-a-boo she'd seen Randall do.

Two men stepped out of the cruiser. Then she took a look at the assault rifle with some type of grenade launcher attached to it. The man wielding the weapon big and broad, dressed in black, and she felt frozen by fear. A moment later there was a steel or aluminum briefcase in his other hand, a large military duffel bag hung around his shoulder, but the man himself had her full attention. She couldn't decide whether to stay put, open the door for them or run like hell out the back, find a deep hole in the canyon and hide. The face was handsome enough, lean and chiseled, but there was something in the way he carried himself as he walked toward her door, his head cocked at an angle toward the Iron County sheriff, whom she had run into three times in the past year.

What was going on? Why was the sheriff looking so bitter and angry? Another glance at the big man and she concluded there was something lethal about him. If he was the Justice agent, then where was Randall? If he wasn't...

"Sally Simpson? I'm Special Agent Michael Belasko."

She watched, felt her heart racing, as he delved into a windbreaker that was rumpled and dusty, as if he'd been rolled down a thousand feet of desert hill and forgot to change clothes. He produced a thin wallet, flipped it open. He held out the ID, toward the window. She felt her cheeks flush, thinking herself stupid, realizing he'd seen her watching him the whole time.

She released the drape, drew a deep breath, trying to will her nerves to smooth out, instead of the jagged charge she felt sparking in her limbs. Somehow she moved. It was the longest few steps to the door she could ever imagine taking. She offered up a silent prayer they weren't her last.

THE SAME FACE OF FEAR and paranoia Randall had worn greeted Bolan again as Sally Simpson opened the door.

"There's been some trouble, Ms. Simpson. I'm afraid your life may be in danger," Bolan said, wanting to get to the next set of problems right away before any black helicopter might sweep over the house. As she took his ID wallet and scoured it with the same skeptical thoroughness that the CBW man had, the Executioner added, "I'm sorry, but Randall's dead."

She pinned Bolan with a look that was somewhere between grief and terror. "What? How?"

"They shot him."

Waterson decided to grab a self-serving moment to confuse and further scare the woman. "This man's a stone-cold killer, ma'am. Don't trust him."

"John Balston is your source at the Justice Department," Bolan quickly said. "I'm going to call the man from Justice who sent me here. If it will ease some tension, he can confirm what you need to know about me." No sale, as she stood, rooted in the doorway, searching Bolan's face. "Listen, if I was here to kill you, I would have done it by now."

She nodded, some of the fear draining from her eyes as she handed Bolan back his ID wallet. "Makes sense to me. Besides, you have the gun. What am I going to do, take it away from you? Come on in."

"After you, Sheriff."

Bolan lagged behind Waterson, gave the sky and the hills a brief search, then walked into Simpson's humble abode.

"So, you're the lady bought old Reb Juperson's home," Waterson said, looking around as if he wanted to sniff his nose at a dwelling that had seen better days. "Hope he got himself enough cash to see him through his retirement in Phoenix."

"He got enough."

"Be seen and not heard, Sheriff," Bolan warned, closing the door. "Take a seat."

"You've seen the black helicopters, haven't you? The men in black?"

Bolan removed his mirrored sunglasses. "You could say we were introduced."

"They tried to kill you, too?" she asked.

"Yeah." Bolan stepped into the small area near the kitchen that passed for a dining room. He laid the briefcase on the table, deposited his war bag on the floor, then dialed the combination that would release the latches to the sat-link. "I came here because Randall thought your life was in danger, and after what I've seen and been through, I believe I need to get you as far away from here as possible."

She moved and stood next to her desk, lit a cigarette, threw Waterson a curious glance, then said to Bolan, "You know about the disk?"

"Yes."

"What's the sheriff's story?"

"He's on their payroll. Or was."

She muttered an oath, shook her head. "If the cops around here are bought by them, we'll never make it out of this county."

"I'm not planning on leaving anytime soon."

She frowned, puzzled. "Meaning what?"

"I suspect you have some idea, after speaking with Randall, what they're doing out there."

"I know it isn't anthrax, or I would have been dead three weeks ago. They post these signs to scare away anyone curious enough to take a stroll near there, warning about anthrax contamination, how they're authorized to use deadly force on trespassers. Same thing I've seen out near Area 51 in Nevada.''

"It's far worse than anthrax, and this isn't any Area 51, if what Randall told me is true. He died because of what he knew, so I tend to believe him.''

She seemed to measure Bolan again, pondering something. "Do you want the disk now?''

"No. First I'm going to call the man who sent me here. Do you want to speak to him?''

She shook her head. "That won't be necessary. I believe you are who you say. You, both of you, do you want something to drink?''

"A glass of ice water would be nice," Bolan said. "Sheriff?''

"A glass of arsenic.''

The soldier read the meanness in the sheriff's tone, sensed Waterson was either on the verge of giving up or making a break for freedom, perhaps believing a Justice Department agent wouldn't shoot him, after all, if he charged for the door. Bolan wouldn't gun him down, but he was determined he would watch the sheriff closely. And he wasn't opposed to some up-close rough stuff if Waterson called the action.

"I'm afraid I don't have any of that, Sheriff.''

"Whiskey, then. Neat.''

"Ms. Simpson," Bolan called out as she went into the kitchen.

"Call me Sally. You're being polite, I think, but all that 'Ms.' business makes me feel like some politically correct libber.''

Bolan smiled to himself, thinking he was lucky

enough to find the lady wasn't going to pull any punches. "Okay, Sally. Is there some place nearby where you can stash your vehicle?"

She stepped back into the doorway, a dark look in her eyes. "Why?"

"A precaution."

"Against what?"

"Those black helicopters."

HAL BROGNOLA SNAPPED up the phone with its secured line on the first ring.

"It's me. I've got big problems out this way."

The big Fed started pacing behind his desk, felt the flush in his face that warned him his blood pressure was going up even more. When the Executioner told Brognola he had big problems, it was cause for the kind of concern that could keep Brognola awake for days, chewing on his nerves until the problems were solved, Bolan style.

For the moment, Brognola was glad his friend had called at all. It was good just to hear his voice, which, of course, always meant Bolan was still alive.

The big Fed had been in his office since he had arranged this strange mission for Bolan last night, contacting his own sources around town, trying to get a handle on any classified military operations in Utah that might cause an alleged CBW scientist to run from the compound in fear for his life. The agonizing wait for Bolan to call back and fill him in had been endured with the help of a pack of antacid tablets, two pots of coffee and hours spent picking the brains of the cyber wizards out at Stony Man Farm.

Brognola noted the edge in Bolan's voice for what

it was. The Stony Man soldier had turned up something solid, perhaps even diabolical, especially if it involved germ or chemical warfare.

"Let's have it, Striker," Brognola said.

And he got it, but it was the kind of report that made Brognola feel as if he were taking a bullet between the eyes. When Bolan finished filling him in, Brognola ground his teeth, well aware of the disaster that was brewing in Utah. What they were doing at the compound wasn't the sort of thing that was supposed to happen in the United States of America. Iraq or North Korea, maybe, but not in a free and democratic society.

"Unbelievable," Brognola said. "Godsbreath? A supervirus? They're testing this on live human subjects? Where the hell do they intend to unleash this horror? When?"

"I haven't found out yet."

"You know, I'm standing here thinking, all the high-tech genius we have at our disposal at the Farm, and they haven't been able to uncover the first clue about what this place is all about. I understand that black projects are funded by the Pentagon, but in most cases involving even black projects, there's something the Farm could hack into, even a file that's buried so deep and so classified it has a million and one codes to crack before it can be broken into and read. They've turned up zip, and that alone spooks the hell out of me. It's one of the few times I can recall the Farm being unable to dig up the first shred of something we need to get the end game in sight."

"It happens to the best of them."

"And to think if this Randall hadn't bolted..."

"No time to dwell on that," Bolan said. "The guy in charge is Roger Paxson. He's ex-Delta. I need everything the Bear can dig up on the man, or maybe you can get hold of his jacket from somebody down at Bragg. He has a small army who seem to do whatever they want, even murder, and get away with it. I smell this guy and his operation as renegade."

"I'll get right on it. What else do you need?"

"I have a sheriff sitting right in front of me I need lifted off my hands."

"Dirty?"

"He was taking Paxson's money. I don't have time to baby-sit."

"I'll scramble up and fly out someone as soon as you sign off."

"Send out a HAZMAT team along with them. Somehow, I'm going to find a way into this place. Whatever's down there is going to need the attention of the best people you can round up. This hell on Earth that Paxson is running out there has to be shut down."

Brognola felt his stomach lurch. "Hold on a second. If you go in, blazing away, and you're exposed to this Godsbreath, Striker..."

"If the compound is built like most classified military installations out here, I have to believe you'll have several levels, vertical shafts leading down, with the hot zone buried at the lowest level. If at all possible, I'll steer clear of the hot zone."

"But, either way, you're taking your chances."

"I don't see where there's a choice, Hal."

"You can wait for the HAZMAT people."

"No can do."

"Damn, but you're bullheaded sometimes, Striker."

"I understand the concern. But I'm looking at three dead state troopers out here, probably killed by Paxson. There's a dead civilian on the highway, a square mile or so of desert covered in bodies, Randall included. Paxson thought he could just blow me and Randall off the highway and be done with it."

"But he's seen now that he's bitten off more than he can chew. Now he's running wild, thinking he might choke on it. Speeding up the game plan."

"Exactly."

Grim, Brognola wondered aloud, "How in God's name can something like this happen in America, Striker?"

"A sign of the times?"

"Yeah. Like Internet kiddie porn and kids with guns?"

"Something like that. Go figure. Only we're looking at a black project that only a few know about, and I'm saying there are some shadows beyond Paxson."

"The Pentagon?"

"You might want to look into it. We've been there before, Hal. Someone in power playing everyone for a fool while they look for some way to gain more power and control. One way or another, I'll have some answers on my end."

Or you'll be dead, Brognola thought. After all the missions he'd seen Bolan survive, he could hardly imagine the man known as the Executioner going out as some freak show struck down and thrashing around in his final moments because of a damn virus.

"Stay in touch," Brognola said.

He knew he didn't have to tell Bolan to stay frosty. He had sent in the best, he knew, and if Bolan couldn't take the compound down, eliminate Paxson, then nothing short of a nuclear strike would end this nightmare.

"I'll call you," Bolan said, and signed off.

Hal Brognola felt his stomach churning as he tried to comprehend the horror of what was actually happening on this mission, the jeopardy his friend was placing himself in, the kind of monsters he was facing down. He set the secured phone back in place, gazed at it and wondered if he'd just heard from Bolan for the last time.

BOLAN SIPPED his ice water, staring at the wall ahead. He couldn't stand to look at Waterson sitting near him, brooding over his fate, sucking down whiskey.

"That's it, Belasko? You just going to hand me over to your people like I'm a common criminal?"

When Bolan didn't answer, he felt Waterson's agitation level rise a few degrees with the heat of anger and resentment.

"I've been a lawman in these parts for twenty years. These people came to me, said they were United States military and needed my services. I would be doing something patriotic for my country. All they wanted was for me to keep an eye on folks, let them know if I overheard any loose talk about their compound. So, they paid me? How many cops you ever met moonlight as security guards, maybe own a restaurant, or sell used cars? Hey, I'm talking to you!"

"Did you ever do it?"

"Do what?"

"Point out anybody to Paxson who might have gotten a little too curious."

The sheriff stared into his empty glass. "Two, maybe three times."

"And after, did you ever see them again?"

Waterson's angry silence told Bolan the truth.

Sally Simpson walked back through the front door. "It's done. I don't even think the black helicopters could find my truck."

"Now what?" Waterson growled. "Hey, missy, I got me an empty glass here. You mind?"

Bolan was considering his next move when the house started shaking as if it would be torn up from its foundation and hurled for the sky. He was up, HK-33 in hand, but Bolan found Waterson was also moving, running straight for the front door.

"Waterson!"

Whether urged on by fear or desperation, Bolan couldn't tell, but he discovered he would never know in the following moments.

Waterson was out the door, barreling over the porch, flapping his arms as the black gunship hovered above the hurricane of dust and rotor wash beyond the sheriff.

The Executioner yelled to the woman, "Come on! Out the back!"

Bolan saw her digging the disk out of a desk drawer, watched Waterson out there waving his arms around as if he were hailing the gunship in for a landing.

The man wasn't only dumb, Bolan thought, but he

was dead on arrival. Paxson wasn't about to leave any loose ends.

The Executioner had seen enough already to know what was coming next. As the soldier hauled up the sat-link and war bag, he glimpsed the 30 mm chain gun in the turret below the cockpit as it opened up in a flash of smoke and fire.

9

"Insiiii..."

The sheriff could have been a traffic cop for all of two seconds, waving toward the living room, shouting at the black helicopter, trying to tell them the ones they wanted were right in front of their gun sights, when the first wave of thundering 30 mm rounds tore his arm off at the shoulder. The appendage all but disintegrated in a reddish-pink cloud, but the gunship was obviously not satisfied with a simple amputation.

Bolan was grabbing Simpson, throwing her to the floor, when he caught his last glimpse of Sheriff Waterson on earth. "Stay down and belly-crawl for the back door! Don't look back and keep moving!" he yelled at Simpson.

If the Tiger Shark was, as Bolan suspected, a bastardized version of the Apache, then the chain gun was capable of pounding out up to 1200 rounds, the stub pylons holding up to sixteen Hellfire missiles. More than enough to bring the house down and spread them clear across the border into Nevada or Arizona, not even enough body pieces to scrape up into a sandwich bag, if anyone even cared to look for what might be left. And the way in which the chopper continued to massacre Paxson's cop clearly told Bolan the Delta man had passed the order down to fire on Waterson with extreme prejudice. Still more indiscriminate slaughter of cops, even a dirty one, and Bolan could well suppose Paxson was over the edge, feeling the squeeze and thus pulling out all the stops, covering his assets no matter who or how many had to go down and stay down.

Waterson jerked under the force of rounds exploding him head to toe, jig stepping all over the porch, his howl of agony drowned as the heavy metal storm went on ripping him up, obliterating the man in one erupting red cloud after another. The overkill lent Bolan several critical heartbeats where he draped his body over the woman, scuttling her for the back door that looked a million miles away in the soldier's grim stare right then.

When Waterson was turned into a vanishing act, nothing but running smears of crimson splotches on the porch, the gunship unleashed the chain gun's wrath on the house. It was a hurricane of earth-moving 30 mm rounds, pounding through wood and stone and hurling glass everywhere at a lightning pace.

Bolan was prepared to make one desperate low charge and bull through the back door when a raking line of 30 mm decimators created a gaping maw in that direction, clearing the way. Every type of home and household debris he could imagine was flaying the air, slashing off his body, the whole foundation shaking as if it were a mobile home being shipped on an 18-wheeler, only slipping off to smash all over the highway. Two, then one more step, fumbling with his gear and assault rifle, and the juggling act carried Bolan out the door as the hellish racket of relentless chain gun fire felt as if it were nailing a spike straight down through his brain.

On the run, the soldier hauled Simpson to her feet when she stumbled and skidded face first to the hard-packed earth. A tornado of rubble swirling around them, he helped her up and then covered her backside with his big frame, urging her to keep running.

"Jump!" she hollered.

He followed her over an edge that seemed to jut out from nowhere. The soldier was unmindful of the slope he glimpsed angling down into a gully, thoughts burning up to only get them to immediate cover. The soldier was forced to trust the woman's judgment they weren't falling far enough to break a leg. The drop was maybe ten feet, the woman landing with acro-batic skill on her backside, sliding up to a stop, her feet impacting with a boulder, bringing her to an abrupt halt. Bolan followed her landing, skidding in on his haunches, the war bag and sat-link taking a beating as they hammered off the hard ground to his flanks.

The Executioner already knew what was coming next. Even though the gunship would blow up the house, Bolan could be sure the killing crew would want to confirm its kills. When they started their search the Executioner would be ready, looking for any opening he could find to bring them down with a surprise package of doom. One shot—that was all he wanted.

Where the slope rose to branch out into some wide crevice at the top and off to his side, Bolan looked up, shuffled over a few feet. He was just in time to catch a few Hellfires wipe the lady's home off the face of the desert. The chopper's gunner wasn't about to leave anything to chance as the soldier watched the home go up, out and gone in a series of boiling fireclouds.

The soldier hauled the Ingram SMG out of the war bag, cocked and locked it. As rubble and flaming shards rained down over the gully, Bolan searched the terrain. It was a scaled-down version of the gorge where he'd earlier taken on Paxson's finest. There appeared a broken maze of deep pockets at the far south edge where she could secure cover and hold on while he took the hunt to the hunters. He wanted her as far away from his next play as possible.

There was no way Bolan would stay put and wait for the opposition to come to him, and there was no point to validating his rescue run of Sally Simpson if he lost her now. Any moment the gunship would fly their way like some giant prehistoric bird hungry for more blood.

"Take it," Bolan told Simpson, holding out the compact SMG, nodding at some point beyond her. "Find a place to hide down at the far end, and don't come out, not even for a quick look. If I don't return, assume the worst, but stay put until they're gone. Do not, under any circumstances, come looking for me."

As if it were something obscene, she reluctantly accepted the subgun.

"All you have to do is point and squeeze the trigger. Aim low. It tends to rise."

"Where are you going?"

Bolan filled the M-203 with an incendiary charge.

"In search of payback for the bastards who just left you homeless."

HAMILTON STARED into the monitor that showed the scientists in level four preparing the test subject. The human guinea pig had just been flown in from LAX, then marched, kicking and screaming, down to level four by three men in black. He was some sort of porn star, Reems, Hamilton believed his name was. A crack addict, with no friends, no family, no money or future. Another nobody, he figured, a subhuman leech the world wouldn't miss. Hell, not even the guy's mother, he thought, could love something like what he saw, a naked, shaking sack of bones, blubbering behind the gag for his life to be spared.

Reems struggled and shed crocodile tears, Hamilton observed, as if his life meant more than that of the President of the United States, or maybe some Einstein who was on the verge of discovering laser or nuclear propulsion that could send space travelers to distant galaxies at light speed. What a schmuck, he decided. Reems would never know that if he died here he would make at least one worthy contribution, a minuscule fragment of atonement for a life of self-indulgence and degradation.

But they never went quietly to the chamber. The porn star was strapped—as they always had to be—to a gurney. Despite the fact he considered any test subjects useless parasites, their tawdry, desperate, impoverished lives simply taking up space and consuming valuable resources, it still bothered Hamilton to watch the horror he knew was about to unfold.

Hamilton had been informed there had been some

minor refinements in the new test vaccine. The CBW team leader, Carlton, said this was perhaps their best shot at a synthetic cure. Hamilton could read into that one-liner, knew it was their last chance to create an antidote to Godsbreath. Given what was happening, all the trouble that had come crashing down on their heads in less than twenty-four hours, Hamilton knew the major was prepared to abandon the compound, take his chances with the suitcase that was already packed and sitting on the metal table in the command center.

Hamilton saw the men in decontamination suits roll the gurney into the chamber, the subject thrashing hopelessly in a vain attempt to break free of the restraints. The scientists injected the porn star with Godsbreath, then another hypodermic—hopefully filled with the magic potion—plunged into the other arm. They lumbered as fast as the decontamination suits would allow, a black-gloved hand hitting the button that shut the airtight, hermetically-sealed door. More shuffling and they were closing off the second door, leaving the porn star alone in the chamber to either live or die the most gruesome death Hamilton had ever witnessed.

It would take two minutes, at least, for the virus and the vaccine to kick in, determine success or failure, life or death.

Hamilton dropped a long stare on the briefcase. Inside were four steel canisters of Godsbreath. Small timers were fixed to each container. They would go off with a muffled pop, something probably not much louder than a firecracker, if the CBW guys had told him the truth during their earlier spiel about the whole package. But the cloud that would be released, to spew up into a fine mist, could kill tens of thousands within a couple of hours. With a good wind to carry the virus, the number of dead could break a hundred thousand in a little over an hour. The most horrifying problem with Godsbreath was that it could be contracted simply by breathing the air it lived in. It wasn't AIDS, where a victim had to come in contact with body fluids, or even Ebola, where close contact was necessary.

No, this virus, invisible to the human eye without significant magnification under a microscope, held the power to perhaps wipe all human life off the face of the earth, send mankind the way of the dinosaurs. Was Hamilton insane to even go this far with the program? Was there some death wish he harbored, a hatred of what he saw happening in his country that cut so deep he was willing to die for it?

In some way, maybe he was like the subjects they duped into coming here. No family to speak of, no firm, stable roots to hold him down at any special place, his whole life having been devoted to either the military or service to Paxson.

Or to the others.

For a moment, he found it incredible that a few shadows, working out of the Pentagon's counter-biological-warfare research program, could have taken it all this far. A few men of power and means, who had created a secret government inside the real government, had cajoled and conned the necessary funding from Congress for this classified project. The legitimate authorities, of course, didn't have the first idea as to what was really going on here, or any clue at all as to what was going to happen soon that would bring the country to a screeching halt, followed, if it went according to plan, by anarchy in the streets. Martial law would be declared when citizens started dropping in the streets from Godsbreath, while Paxson, himself and a few others held the White House, the President and all his men hostage.

It would be the coup of all time. The problem would be living long enough, outside a decontamination suit, to taste the fruit of victory, marshal up all branches of the Armed Forces under their command by using the threat of Godsbreath to take down American cities and towns. Soldiers would weed out the radicals and rebels, all the dregs and whoever else the chosen deemed unfit to live in their New World Order. Mass executions, extermination of entire targeted segments of American society would be the order of the day to crush the anticipated countrywide rebellion. Later on, when their program was rolling like the juggernaut they envisioned, it wouldn't really matter who was shot. Race, color and creed would be overlooked for the greater good of the New America. If they wouldn't submit, become slaves for the great American labor force, they were dead, plain and simple.

Impossible? Insane? he thought. Not really. They lived in crazy times anyway, the signs of insanity in American society everywhere, screaming in the faces of rational and moral men on a daily basis. The masses, with their drugs and guns and lust for pleasure and money, had simply become barbarians beating down the gates of civilization. And all future obstacles, seemingly insurmountable or otherwise, would be overcome by sheer force of brutal and decisive action.

Or the threat of Godsbreath.

It was happening in the chamber, Hamilton saw, fast and awful, as it always did. He twisted a knob on the control panel, zoomed in for a close-up on the porn star. Convulsions were the first symptom. Then the victim's eyes rolled back in the skull, leaving only two bugging white orbs that looked set to pop out of their sockets. Sweat broke out from every pore, as if the skin from head to toe were just a series of leaky faucets. Hamilton watched as the fever kicked in, the whole raging firestorm inside the body began bursting blood vessels, unleashing bloody ooze from every orifice, the blood boiling so hot so fast it appeared like oil as it ran out of ears, nose, anus. He watched, felt his horror growing, then experienced a stab of fear twisting in his gut.

If the vaccine was going to work, it would have happened by now.

Maybe next time. There were still two homeless men, picked up from the Hollywood streets, waiting in the wings. But Hamilton suspected the project had reached its conclusion with the porn star. Paxson was calling the shots, after all, and he'd already implied it was time to wrap it up here and move on to the next phase.

Hamilton panned the monitor back to Carlton, who was already looking up at the camera. No, Hamilton didn't need to see him shaking his head to know they were looking at yet another failure. In a minute or so, the flame-thrower above the gurney would wash white phosphorous over the body, a blinding wall of cleansing flame that would appear to swell the chamber so that it looked ready to burst through the hermetically sealed bubble. The chamber would next undergo another period of purification, a long decontamination stage with formaldehyde and whatever other decontaminants he believed they might use but didn't care to know about.

Grim, he looked away from the monitor, his dark stare falling on the suitcase. Paxson had raised him thirty minutes ago with news of the disaster on the desert. The major was on the way back, expecting some bright light to shine, wash a glimmer of hope over their problems.

Hamilton heard his angry chuckle echo through the room. He only hoped the major could endure yet another round of bitter frustration without flying off into a mindless rage. A display that could catch anybody in the man's gun sights.

Hamilton hoped Paxson didn't flip out so much that he became a source of blame, the first shooting target on the spot when more bad news was announced.

RISING PLUMES of black smoke and shimmering walls of fire veiled the XH-10 Tiger Shark. It was lifting off, swinging out from its position to assume a hovering position above the destruction.

The Executioner stayed low, HK-33 gripped tight and ready to cut loose as he watched the gunship slowly spin around, edge forward and lift a few feet up over the wall of fire.

If this killing crew played true to the numbers of the previous Tiger Shark, the soldier figured one M-60 door gunner, a pilot and copilot. That no reinforcements had swarmed the scene, ground or air, was a positive sign he might seal their doom and quickly evacuate with Simpson in one piece.

Whatever his next course of action beyond here, well, it was on hold.

First the gunship.

Rotor wash was sweeping some of the smoke away from the flaming heap that had marked the woman's home. The soldier slid farther down along the rise, hugging the jagged lip, angling deeper away from the tail rotor, wanting to make his charge in from their back—and their blind side. Helicopters, no matter how sophisticated with high-tech genius, didn't sport side view mirrors.

They were holding their position inside, most likely now searching for any signs of life. It made perfect sense, the only thing to do, and their watching urged him on.

The chopper lowered a few feet, and Bolan saw a man hop out of the fuselage doorway, on the far side. The hardman fanned the lake of fire with his HK MP-5 subgun, as if expecting some flaming scarecrow to come charging out of there. The gunner kept his back turned to Bolan, and the soldier knew he'd never get a better chance, gauging the distance at something around twenty yards.

The Executioner broke over the rise, eyelids slitting against the dust storm as he bulled into the machine-made hurricane. He was counting on his first burst being nothing more than a sound like a few firecrackers popping off, hoping by the time the flyboys figured out the noise for what it was he would be in the fuselage, in their face, or standing outside and winging an incendiary hellbomb their way.

He was charging past the tail end, his HK-33 drawing target acquisition, trying to shave down a few more necessary steps before firing when suddenly the hardman wheeled his way. Bolan let him have it with three 5.56 mm rounds, stitching him across the chest, kicking him into the fire he had seemed so mesmerized by a second before.

If they'd heard or seen it, the men in the gunship didn't show any sign of either awareness or panic over their fallen comrade.

Bolan bounded up into the fuselage, surged past the bolted-down and belted M-60. On the charge, he changed the play in midstride, determined to take it to the flyboys, up close and personal, ensure the grim finality. A black helmet turned his way, a mouth whipping around into view and gaping over the minimike near his lips, when Bolan held back on the trigger and blew the look of surprise and anger off the pilot's face in a disfiguring crimson facial no mortician could ever fix up for suitable presentation to a weeping audience of friends and family.

It was set to go to hell in the next few heartbeats as the soldier veered a few steps across the floor, hosing the cockpit with a long burst of autofire. He believed he caught a shout of rage, maybe a scream of pain somewhere beyond the din of his weapon spitting out its fusillade of lead. Hard to tell, but not that it made any real difference now that he was on a roll. The Executioner's sweeping autofire drilled a few wild rounds into the instrument panel and sent sparks flying around the cockpit, while still more streaks of blood hit the Plexiglas. The copilot came jumping from his seat only to start dancing around as the lead tumblers chopped him up. He was toppling over the control panel, sliding down over the throttle, when his convulsing death throes began hitting the control sticks, pitching the chopper.

The floor was leaning up before Bolan, but he was already racing for the door. On the fly, the soldier leaped out the doorway, sailed down the few feet to a hard landing. Catching his balance, the soldier pivoted and tapped the M-203's trigger. This was one bird he didn't want to see rise again. He dropped the incendiary round into the cockpit. As the white flash erupted in the corner of his sight, Bolan sprinted from the unmanned chopper. A look back, as the ball of white fire seared out of the cockpit, then Bolan scrambled for cover, hurling himself over the edge of the rise. The gunship hammered down on its nose, rising into a sort of impromptu stand on its turret, then was flipped over by its own angry momentum, slamming down on its main rotors.

The woman's safety burned into Bolan's thoughts. He hoped Simpson hugged her cover, didn't cave to fear or some curious impulse to check the immediate area that was set to blow up into a firestorm. He knew the woman was far down at the deep end of the gully, buried well inside a pocket, but if she peeked out…

What came next cranked up the risk factor, though, threatening anyone, covered or not, within a hundred-yard radius or more of the explosion. The soldier tumbled down into a ring of boulders, braced himself, covering his head, as he heard the screech of housing coming apart, the shrieking of rotor blades slashing off the earth. With nowhere to spin freely, they were torn into giant steel fingers that flew over Bolan's position. Searing flames reached out for the soldier but somehow shot overhead, strips of wreckage banging off the rock wall directly across the gully. The ground under Bolan shuddered, seemed to ripple even with each sound of rolling thunder. Maybe thirty yards away, he heard the groaning of steel, the hull breaking apart, warped and punched out by the fireballs. The flaming sharkbird rolled over the rise, took a slow-motion roll down the slope, spewing out more razoring hunks of steel before it settled on its side in a crunch. A giant billow of dust and a searing mass of flames marked the chopper's final resting place.

The Executioner was out and climbing for the rise. Topping the ridge, he ran, surging through the trailing shroud of black smoke, the stench of burning fuel and toasted flesh surrounding him. Another rush of adrenaline kept the hope pounding in his heart. It seemed the longest run yet on this mission, as he sprinted, closing the gap to her cover.

"Sally! Sally, it's safe now!" he shouted down into the gully.

He was descending the slope when she came into Bolan's sight, the woman easing out of the pocket with what appeared great reluctance. She gripped the Ingram, staring up at the soldier as he trooped down the final few steps, then pulled up and searched her face. She was shaking, unsure of her surroundings, as she turned and stared past Bolan, toward the roaring bonfire.

The soldier gently took back the Ingram subgun. "Sally, look at me. Are you all right?"

She gave him a shaky nod. "Yes. Now...now what?"

"Your vehicle, go get it. I'll meet you up top. It's finished here."

She malingered, then broke free of her paralysis. She trudged off on trembling legs, but picked up the pace with each forward step. Watching the brave lady, Bolan could only imagine what she was enduring— the horror of men dying sudden violent deaths in her presence, not to mention anguish over losing her home, now finding herself swept up in the madness of an enemy hunting to kill her—but there was no time to soothe bad nerves, hand out false promises. All Bolan felt was an urgent need to put some quick distance to the hellzone.

The Executioner retraced his steps to his war bag and sat-link, grateful to find both items were untouched during the Tiger Shark's raging demise. Round two was under the belt, a few more men no longer at Paxson's command. But the Executioner knew he'd only hurled more fuel to fan the flames of his enemy's angry determination.

And what Bolan had in mind next would send him marching straight into the fires of Paxson's Hell on Earth, if he could find a way in.

10

Mitch Targon massaged his aching breastbone. He considered another attempt at smoking, then told himself to forget it. It was hard enough to even draw a normal breath, much less a nice deep one on the butt end of a Camel. Two previous tries at a smoke had seen him gnashing his teeth, cursing up a storm when the pain started shooting daggers through his lungs, the smoke hacked back out of his mouth like some teenager's coughing fit on a first-ever cigarette. Targon wanted to maintain himself in front of his comrades, a show of balls, allowing him to cling to damaged machismo while he sucked it up and rode it out. Try as he might, though, he couldn't will away the searing fire that would fan out to lance his rib cage with so many white-hot needles he knew he could forget any more Camels for the next few days, perhaps even a week.

So he suffered in silence for the moment, watching Benson and Hurley chain-smoke, the two of them again puffing up big fat clouds in the living room of their mobile home—which doubled as a command post—in Camellion. He couldn't be positive what they thought about the ass-whipping he'd been handed, but he could be sure he wouldn't like it one bit if they were somehow replaying the scene in their heads, grateful only that it was him who'd taken the lumps, leaving them to carry on in their image of themselves as the toughest black ops the CIA had ever trained and put in the field. Considering what they'd seen at the motel, he hated them for even being there, heads tilting his way now and then, sure their eyes were walking over him behind their mirrored shades, judging him.

As if it were his fault the guy had escaped in the first place to run amok and start waxing Paxson's soldiers, blowing gunships out of the sky, piling up the bodies and wreaking more havoc by the hour. At least he could take it, he thought, get up, brush off the dust and want nothing more than some righteous payback while the smug pricks sat there, holding him in what he believed was silent contempt.

Gingerly he rubbed his chest again. Beneath the thin cotton black pullover, the angry black-and-purple bruise, about the size of a softball, proved a constant reminder of his shame, delivered at the hands of one flunky from the Justice Department, no less.

Only if the reports they'd received from first Paxson and then Hamilton were to be believed, this guy was serious stiff opposition. It made him wonder if the bastard was even an agent from the Justice Department. No G-man he'd ever seen or heard of had the kind of martial talent, the kick-ass way they'd been hearing about, whenever, of course, Hamilton or Paxson deemed them worthy enough to raise on the radio for an update or receive further orders.

"How come Hamilton handed off this detail to the three of us?" Targon groused, believed his voice came out scratchy, maybe even a little on the squeaky side, since he could still feel the bastard's fingers that had dug into his windpipe like a vise. "If you ask me, it's lackey work. Is there some message here I'm missing?"

"We're the only ones who aren't Delta, that's my guess," Benson said, blowing out a long cloud of smoke by the wet bar, looking his HK MP-5 over for the third time, even though he'd already stripped and cleaned it an hour ago.

"You're wrong, and what the hell difference would that make?" Targon said, coughed, caught Benson and Hurley glance at each other. Was that a sneer on Benson's lips? "Six others are standard Army issue. Then you have two Rangers."

"What's your point?" Hurley asked, but sounding as if he didn't care about an answer one way or the other. He was busy playing solitaire on the dining-room table, not even bothering to look up from his cards.

"My point is maybe Paxson's pointing fingers of blame our way. We've been singled out, isolated from the rest."

"He could have left us stranded, ordered us to watch the motel while he choppered out the others. Now, that would have been certain pointless surveillance detail. At least a man was dispatched to deliver us some wheels," Benson pointed out.

"Cleanup, that's all it was," Targon growled, stifling another fit of coughing, holding his ground in the middle of the living room. "They had those vehicles hooked to a tow and rolled up into that 18-

wheeler before we were even hopping into another unmarked.''

Hurley heaved a breath. ''What do you want me to say? Paxson wants us to sit tight and alert him the second we see this Belasko.''

''That's *if* he even shows here,'' Targon said. ''For all we know he's packed it in. He's drawn his first blood, maybe figures it's more a hassle now than it's worth. He's probably back behind his desk in D.C.''

''That's not the read I took from Hamilton,'' Benson said. ''He said there's been trouble, gave me a few of the particulars. This Justice guy doesn't strike me as some paper pusher or desk jockey. It's turned ugly out there in the desert. Indications are the trouble could be headed our direction. He said yet another of their prized gunships hasn't checked back in, this after confirmation of another sighting of Mr. Justice. Now, we have eyes and ears here in Camellion. If he's headed this way, maybe he thinks he'll get some help here, then the phone will ring and we're back in the game.''

''It bugs me, all this hanging around.'' Targon paced, fingering the butt of his shoulder-holstered Beretta 92-F. ''You'd think Paxson would have put us back out there in the hunt. I mean, I think we deserve a little more respect. You remember Panama, gentlemen? Without us handing over critical intelligence to Delta, Noriega would have slipped through Uncle Sam's fingers.''

''Maybe Paxson doesn't live in the glory days.''

Targon pinned Benson with an angry eye. ''What the hell's that mean?''

"Settle down. If he shows he shows. If he walks into Camellion, bold as brass, you'll have your shot."

"That what you think I'm all about?"

"Take it easy. Why are you getting so defensive?" Hurley said.

"Why? Because I was the one at the door who nearly had my throat ripped out by this bastard. His foot felt like it went right through my chest. I want this guy's ass, no, I want to shoot him where it won't kill him. I want to see him beg for his life before I chop his head off and take it back and dump it at Paxson's feet."

They didn't look impressed by his angry spiel, remaining fixed to their own distractions, as if he hadn't even spoken.

Targon strode for the front door. "Yeah, you two keep on playing with yourselves."

"Where are you going?" Hurley asked.

"I need some fresh air."

"Don't go too far."

"Kiss my ass," he growled.

Targon stepped outside into a blast of heat. The sun was going down, but it didn't feel any cooler. The rows of mobile homes off to his side were hit by the shadows rolling in from the surrounding desert. Soon it would be dark, and the place the locals referred to as Spookville would live up to its billing. Camellion would appear a solemn outpost in the middle of nowhere, no one venturing outside after dark, the place that was a retreat for government workers in the area looking a ghost town by all outward appearances. If the bastard was coming in at all, Targon was sure he would cloak himself in darkness.

Why wait for the Fed to show? Targon looked at their black unmarked vehicle, considered taking it out to the desert, thinking he might get lucky and catch the agent stumbling around on foot. Then he saw the blind behind him pulled back an inch or so, Hurley standing there, peering at him from behind his shades, as if the guy was reading his mind. Screw both of them, he thought. Soon enough he'd pursue some personal course of action, which right then included a trip to the bar for a couple belts of whiskey to ease the pain. A few minutes of peace and quiet away from their silent contempt. It was a long shot anyway, the Fed showing up here, but he was keeping his fingers crossed. One clean shot was all he wanted, just one more chance, and he could redeem himself. Stranger things had happened here in Camellion, so one more dead body whisked out of the place wouldn't raise too many eyebrows. He thought about the sudden disappearances of government workers, never seen or heard from again. There had been several accidental deaths over the past six months, loose tongues made silent in the middle of the night. It was wetwork, of course, and he'd played no small part in some of the stranger and more ominous accidents in Camellion.

As he walked down the middle of the street, angling away from their command post, which was tucked at the far south end of the prefab town, he could feel their eyes watching him from behind the blinds of their air-conditioned enclaves. The unseen perhaps wondering if they had slipped up, said something to a neighbor they shouldn't have, maybe now checking under the beds for a western rattlesnake, or looking around the toilet seat for a thin wire that would betray a hookup to a black box, ready to fry them from a long jolt of lethal voltage. When Paxson let some of his workforce step outside the mountain compound, granting them a little R and R, trying to look the benevolent boss, this was where they breathed the outside air. The major might be hooked up with some clout and connections to other classified military operations in the area, allowing his tired workers to mingle here, but there was always the danger of a careless or frightened tongue when the working masses got together.

Enter Mitch Targon.

All the quiet kills, he thought, the dirty work he'd done for Paxson that no one beyond his small circle would ever know about.

Silently he urged the agent to show up. He was ready to take credit for one kill that wouldn't be silent at all. In fact, he hoped they heard the guy's screams all the way back to the compound.

He wanted the guy's head, and with the bastard's blood on his hands he would win back respect.

"DO YOU HAVE any friends here?" Bolan asked.

"No," she said, guiding the SUV across another vast and empty stretch of desert.

Bolan searched the desolation, didn't spot a sign of life—not man, animal or machine—in any direction. He clung to the hope that Randall was right about Paxson having only two gunships. Just the same, the HK-33 was canted against his seat, a full clip in place, a 40 mm frag grenade fed into the M-203.

"Boyfriend?"

"No."

"Family?"

"No."

"Anybody?"

"Look, after the divorce I moved out here to get away from people, all the rat race that came with the city. I know what you're trying to ask me. You want to dump me off at somebody's doorstep like some charity case, so you can go after Paxson without having to lug me along as baggage."

Bolan looked away from the lady, felt the weary smile on his lips. She was a looker, a head-turner he couldn't believe anybody would ever consider baggage. Given her stubborn display, Bolan was starting to believe getting her safely out of harm's way might prove a time-consuming chore, rife with more argument and hassle and protest on both sides than he could afford to wade through. He was on Paxson's clock, and he could already hear the doomsday numbers ticking down.

The sat-link was in the soldier's lap, opened up. If he didn't hear from Brognola in the next few minutes, he needed to call back, take whatever the big Fed had on Paxson. If by chance Paxson escaped the soldier here in Utah, he needed some point of reference, some direction in which he could resume the hunt. It didn't matter if the Executioner wanted to end it here or not. Paxson was licking his wounds, knew the walls were closing in, could bail at any time. What if he had some vials of Godsbreath ready for dispersal? What if he was hell-bent on stepping up the timetable for whatever he had in mind and was even then already flying away from the compound. Worst-case scenario was for Paxson to disappear to parts unknown, not a clue as to where he might be headed next.

"I won't have your blood on my conscience, Sally."

"You won't."

"You can't be sure of that."

"I've seen your work, don't forget."

"Maybe I just got lucky, or they were careless."

"I don't think so."

"There will be a next time."

"I'm safest right by your side."

"I can't have it."

"There's nowhere for me to go, no one I can trust."

"At Camellion I can put in a call to the nearest state police barracks. They'll round you up."

She frowned. "And you'll be on your marauding way."

"Marauding isn't exactly what's going to happen."

"Whatever. Listen to me, please. What if Paxson has a few more cops in his pocket like the good sheriff? I don't especially get all warm and fuzzy when I see myself marched by a corrupt state trooper into some dark room, shot once in the head and then buried in an unmarked grave out in the desert."

"Paxson murdered three of their own. I don't think he has any state cops on his payroll."

She shot Bolan a defiant look. "I've given you the disk, so now you're going to just brush me off?"

"Call it what you want."

"Brush-off. Listen, I stay by your side, that's it."

"Or I can get out now."

She sighed, took a moment to choose the words for

her next path of protest. "At least leave me behind
when you go do whatever it is you're going to do,
but keep me close enough to wherever you're going.
Stashed away, you've seen I'm pretty good at staying
put. I'm not giving myself up to risk some awful turn
of fate, troopers, folks at Camellion, whoever. Look,
you came and got me, you want to make sure I'm
safe, so don't let me too far out of your sight and lose
me now. Besides, if you're thinking about taking a
look at the compound I know a way in that will get
you close enough without getting spotted by cameras,
motion sensors or whatever else they use for surveillance. At least, so far that I could see. All I know is
the times I've been out there at night, I haven't been
chased away. I've found a hole in their armor. You
need me."

Bolan had to admit her argument made sense, but
that didn't mean he had to buy it. Still she made several good points. And there was no time to spare forcing his own protests on her, find her safe haven and
wait for the cops to show up, the woman explaining
situations the police wouldn't buy until they had one
Special Agent Belasko snatched up and cooling his
heels in a cell.

The soldier nodded. "Okay. But you'll do what I
say when I say."

"You're in charge."

"Just get us close to Camellion."

"You never told me why you want to go there."

Bolan suddenly heard the buzzing signal on his sat-
link, picked up the receiver. "Yeah."

"Paxson has his own pharmaceutical company,
Striker," Brognola said, the note of urgency in the

big Fed's voice coming through, loud and clear, over the satellite link. "Dallas. They have a central office there, research laboratory, warehouse for distribution, the works. They're FDA approved, you can even buy some stock in the company. They're on the New York Stock Exchange even, nothing that would set a guy up for life maybe, but the impression they give is they're legit.

"Bragg's not talking about Paxson, they damn near hung up on me in midsentence. The Bear will hack into their files and get me his jacket, but you can bet whatever he's done for Uncle Sam is classified, probably not the first piece of paper on the guy. Deny everything is all we'll get on Paxson."

"So, forget Bragg. We know enough about the guy already to know he has to be shut down."

"Well, I'm sure it goes without saying, but you have my blessing to nail this bastard. Okay, Aaron has turned up a number of his business associates in the Dallas area. Doctors, a few military and business types. I can fax you a shopping list in the next few minutes. Looks like Paxson has pretty much covered what he needs to make inroads into the medical field. My guess would be they have their own private distributors, probably peddle your basic household prescriptions, shipped out to mostly local hospitals, pharmacies, what have you. Smoke screen, all of it, and if it isn't I'll turn in my resignation tomorrow."

"I'm pretty sure you won't have to go that far."

"I appreciate the vote of confidence."

"Always. So, if Paxson's running his own pharmaceutical company, it wouldn't be too difficult for him to obtain, even have a team put together the necessary ingredients, using precursor chemicals, to start his own bio- or chem-warfare program.''

"The Bear's working on it, but the trail looks blurred already.''

"What's the company's claim to fame?''

"Glad you asked me that. Hold on, because here's the clincher. When you first mentioned the guy's name, I knew I'd heard of Paxson somewhere. I saw him on CNN about two months ago, Striker, in the White House, shaking the President's hand.''

Bolan heard the alarm bells ringing in his head.

"I hear the silence speaking angry volumes, Striker. I just woke up a few sleeping beauties around town who were at the meeting. Get this. Paxson has the Man's ear, claims his research team is on the verge of a major breakthrough in the treatment of AIDS, perhaps even a cure. Some sort of announcement is set to be made in three days. And none other than ex-Delta Force Major Paxson has a meeting scheduled with the Man in the Oval Office. There will be prime-time interruption. Cable and everybody else from Dan Rather on down the line will be there to cover this supposed announcement of a miracle breakthrough.''

"I'm getting a real bad feeling on where this is headed, Hal.''

"I've been juggling three phones for forty-five minutes, not to mention staying on-line with the Farm while Aaron sweated and cursed his way to get me what we've got so far. Don't hold back now if you have a hunch.''

"The announcement, I'm thinking, is Paxson's ticket to the Man. I'm thinking he plans to carry a

few vials of this Godsbreath right into the Oval
Office.''

Brognola cursed. "And do what?"

"I can't say."

"Hold the President as a hostage? Take down the
White House using Godsbreath as blackmail? To
what end?"

"I can't be one hundred percent sure. But it would
fit the guy's basic sociopathic style. Human life is
simply an obstacle if it keeps him from getting whatever it is he wants. What the end game is, I couldn't
tell you."

"So, we need to start raising a few drawbridges on
Paxson."

"Wake up the President, Hal, have that meeting
canceled. Have some of your people stake out the
Dallas connection. I'm betting Paxson is going to bail
here. If he turns up in Dallas, just have your people
watch him."

"You're going into the compound, aren't you?"

The fear in the big Fed's voice didn't escape Bolan.
"No other play left. The eleventh hour is in my
face."

"I've arranged for a team of blacksuits from the
Farm and a HAZMAT team to be flown in to Hill Air
Force Range. That's a little north of where you'll be,
and I'm looking at 24:00 tops before they can chopper
to the site."

"No time to wait on the cavalry."

"You realize once, even if, you get inside…"

"I understand the risks involved. To finish your
thought, yeah, I may not come out."

"Damn it, Striker, there has to be another way."

"Not from where I sit." Quickly Bolan ran down the Sally Simpson situation. "Before I make my move on the compound, I'll raise the blacksuits on standby back at Cedar City."

"And have them pick her up?"

"She'll have the disk on her," he said, and caught the lady throwing him a mixed look of anger and curiosity. "I'm setting a time frame for once I go in. I'm not out by then, the blacksuits will fly her and the disk back your way."

Brognola heaved a long breath on the other end. "Anything else I need to worry about?"

"I think you have enough on your hands already. This thing is gathering momentum, a life of its own, Hal, and it's getting stronger with each passing minute."

"As in Godsbreath. I don't even want to imagine what could happen if—"

"So, don't. I'll handle it on my end, just have the way paved for me if a few of them escape my sights. You can bet Paxson has some sort of contingency plan. He's boxed in, but if he wiggles out, I need to be in his face before he has time to take another breath."

"You'll have what you need if the guy flies on. Good luck, Striker."

"I'll call you," Bolan said, and signed off.

"They've created a doomsday virus. Am I right?"

Bolan didn't answer the lady right away, his thoughts turned to his next move. He needed a way into the compound, and he was betting his best chance was someone placed by Paxson in Camellion as a watchdog.

"I want you to tell me anything you know about Camellion," Bolan said.

She nodded at the low chain of jagged hills to the west. "It's just beyond there. What? You plan on just walking right into town?"

"Something like that."

"And do what?"

"I'm betting Paxson left some eyes there. I need a way into the compound. A swipe card, a hostage, I'll take whatever I can get."

"You never answered my question."

Bolan looked at the lady. "Yes. They've created a doomsday virus."

11

"Kragen, Barber and Braxton, you'll be flying with me."

Paxson counted fifteen men, including Hamilton, sitting at the long conference table in the war room. Minus the three he'd take with him to Dallas, then on to Washington, that left twelve guns to carry out his orders, then tackle whatever opposition might come hunting for them.

And their adversary? he thought, choking down his rage before he reached out and started crushing throats, looking for any release for his bitter frustration. It galled him to even think that one man had nearly cut his hardforce in half, leaving him with pretty much a skeleton crew to carry out the final act here. The loss of men on the battlefield was always bad enough, even though a professional soldier knew the risks when faced with armed opposition, aware that sudden death could take him out of the fight at any time. But the fact that one man had taken them down made Paxson wonder about morale. They looked hard and determined enough, appeared ready to follow up his orders at first scrutiny, but there was something behind the eyes of a few of his people that made him wonder if they perhaps were losing their nerve, might even question the orders. He had just given them the word, but to make sure everyone was crystal clear on what was expected, he repeated himself.

"Terminate everyone, that includes the labor detail. Set the charges and blow them on your way out the door. Use white-phosphorous charges for level four. Once beyond the wall, more charges to bring the mountain down over the front gate." He was standing but he leaned down, put his hands on the edge of the table, eyeballing each man in turn. "Check your watches. Hamilton will call the workers for a meeting in one hour. They will be gathered in the mess hall, waiting for you. Shouldn't be too difficult. Quick and clean, then you're on your way, gentlemen. Any questions?"

Paxson waited, watching them shake their heads. "When it's done, gentlemen, you will be choppered to Nellis. I will expect to see you in Washington late tomorrow night. Dismissed."

The steel door opened and Paxson waited until they filed out, the last man shutting the door behind him, leaving him alone with Hamilton.

"Something bothering you, Hamilton?"

"One man has us packing it in, so, yes, I'm a little disturbed."

"What, exactly, disturbs you? That I'm flying on, leaving you to clean up here."

Hamilton sat like a statue, staring at his hands. "Everyone knows your name by now. I don't see how we'll pull it off."

"They don't know shit. And even if they do think they know something, I'll still have the containers. I see where you're headed with this. All right, say the meeting with the President is canceled. Say the Justice Department or the FBI uses all available manpower to search me out and try to nail me. I scrap Plan A, that's all. Find a hotel, maybe the Marriott by the Key Bridge where I always stay when I'm in D.C. I always liked the view of the town from that restaurant up top anyway. Then all I need is a rooftop, a cellular phone and a little wind at my back. Are you afraid, after what's happened here, our people in Washington aren't going to back us? Is that the problem?''

''With what's happened, if they fear exposure, yes, they may bail. Or even send out their own headhunters.''

''Then I'll take them down, too. Worst case—I blackmail the White House, get us a nice chunk of change and we'll just skip the country. Our people turn on us, they'll find they've grabbed the bull by the horns. End of story.''

''What about our business with the Iranians?''

''That's another matter I have to straighten out.''

''They paid half already—they'll expect delivery.''

''The nerve gas is in Dallas, drummed up, ready to fly. But the way things stand now, it might be too risky to conclude the deal. We needed them as an overseas connection in case things went south here in the States, but that's just one reason why I groomed them from the beginning. We used them, my thinking was we could always start over on the other side of the world. I'll touch base with the Iranians as soon as I'm in the air. They were scheduled to fly into Dallas today. I'm thinking they might prove another loose end I need to tie up. Hey, we knew this day might come when we had to shut down, leave a bunch of bodies behind. Because of one man or a hundred men, it doesn't matter, our operation is finished here.

"Now, if there's nothing else, I believe I need to get on that jet. I'll be expecting you in Dallas by morning."

Paxson watched Hamilton closely as the man stood and walked off. Was that doubt he'd read in Hamilton's eyes? Fear? Hamilton went out the door in the next moment, taking with him whatever bad vibes Paxson sensed.

SALLY SIMPSON WATCHED the man she knew as Belasko shadow up on the back side of the nearest mobile home. He was toting the military-type duffel bag, the kind that could fit half a parking lot inside, she thought. The bag reminded her briefly of the day her ex-husband had stuffed whatever wasn't nailed down in their home into just such a bag. That was where any similarities between Belasko and the ex ended.

Before he ventured any farther, she figured he'd ditch the bag, his hands free to inflict whatever damage he intended on the opposition. One second he was there in her sight; the next moment he was gone, vanishing like a ghost, the man moving like some great cat as he took his hunt to the last mobile home at the opposite end of the main dirt road. Down there, a black car stood out among the SUVs in Camellion, and she'd noted the grim interest Belasko had shown the vehicle before moving off. She suspected he was going after what he hoped was his ticket into the compound. She wasn't sure what he planned to do in Camellion, or beyond—the man telling her next to nothing—but after witnessing Belasko's grim work she could venture a good guess that whoever was in the target mobile home was about to get a bad taste of his heavy-hitting style. The man was something to watch, the way he took charge….

What was she thinking anyway? Some other time, another place, and she might entertain romantic ideas about Belasko. Tall, dark and handsome, he sure fit that bill and in the strictest sense. She knew he was a killer, but he was hardly some psychopathic slaughter machine. No, there was something else about the man, something real, that both intrigued and puzzled her. There was integrity about Belasko, a character, she believed, that could never be questioned, his life and values not for sale. She wondered for a moment who the man really was, thinking he was something other than an agent for the Justice Department. As far as she knew, it wasn't standard operating procedure for the Justice Department to send one agent out in the field. It didn't matter how good the agent was; it just seemed to buck the norm. Then again, everything she'd seen in the past day was like one of those bizarre stories she might have written for the tabloids. Secret military bases. Men in Black. Gunships. And the clincher was that she now knew what they were doing out there in the mountain base. No, the truth hadn't set her free, she thought, not by a long shot. The reality, in fact, was so terrifying that to even know she was on the same continent with a doomsday virus had her conjuring up images of people dying slow, horrible deaths all across America. Faces maybe bubbled up with blisters, oozing sores all over bodies that were twitching like puppets on a string, as the dead convulsed in the streets of major American cities, piling up, to be put to the torch by armed soldiers in decontamination suits. The military forcing thousands of civilians into quarantine, herding them up like so much cattle, small-town America turned into a death camp—

Stop it, she told herself, hold on and hope Belasko was the man to derail and crush these architects of death.

So she sat behind the wheel of her SUV, doors locked as he had instructed, nothing to do but wait for him to return. Her vehicle was parked on a rise, north of Camellion, engine off. The first of several generator-powered lights was blinking on from the thin lampposts that were planted at staggered intervals down the main street bisecting the facing rows of mobile homes. She found herself staring at the black car, some suspicious thought wanting to take shape in her mind, not sure why the vehicle sitting there, alone and waiting for Belasko to do whatever, bugged her so much all of a sudden.

Again he'd left the compact submachine gun behind, and she gave the weapon a long look, wondering if she could—no, would—use it if her life was threatened. He was explicit in that level, take-charge voice of his. The first sign of trouble and she was to roll down into Camellion, start banging on doors, scream bloody murder, the weapon to be used only as a last resort.

It hit her like a bolt of lightning. "You son..."

The duffel bag. The black car. Once he snatched whoever was at the end of his stalk, he intended to ditch her.

"No way, Belasko," she said, feeling a surge of anger that he would so casually ditch her. It didn't matter if he thought he was doing it for her own good. She had a stake in his problems, his mission, the way she saw it. She had lost her home and the few personal possessions that had marked what she viewed as an obscure life. But they had been her things; it had been her home they had taken from her. There was nothing left for her in Utah, she decided with sudden grim determination, but to see this trouble through to its conclusion. Forget the ambition of revealing to the world the truth about the supervirus. When they had leveled her home into smoking rubble, it had turned personal. And she wanted to see Belasko nail them.

She was reaching for the key, but decided to give it a few minutes before turning on the engine and driving down into Camellion.

"You're not getting rid of me that easily."

THE EXECUTIONER CROUCHED behind a mobile home. Three more of the clonelike structures down, and he intended to go through the back door, in and out, quick and clean, if possible. He needed a live one, though, someone who carried a magnetic swipe card. If there was a code that went along with the card, he could get it from whoever was on the receiving end of his business here.

Or else figure out another way into the compound.

He set the war bag on the ground, not planning to leave it behind any longer than necessary, aware that when he soon hit the desert compound he would need every last clip of ammunition and grenade at his disposal. The HK-33 was stowed away in the bag, his weapon of choice at the moment the Beretta 93-R. He took a few seconds to assess his next move, threaded the sound suppressor to the Beretta's muzzle.

This retreat—or whatever Camellion really was—had a sterile look and feel about it. Spooky, all right. Whoever had housed these people here and why, Bolan reckoned it was most likely a way for the upper echelons to plant spies, weed out any loose tongues who might feel the need to talk about their classified work out here. It struck him as Gestapo-esque, but after what he'd seen so far during this campaign, nothing surprised him anymore. Not that it mattered in the final analysis. He was there to make some noise, if forced to, rattle their somber world some more. The temporary residents may or may not have seen him walk in, but Bolan had no choice but risk being spotted by watching eyes.

A quick look back at the way he'd come in, and he hoped Simpson would stay put until he bagged a prisoner and commandeered the black four-door vehicle. The lady may or may not figure out she was being abandoned, but she had become a liability. Short of taking her straight to the nearest state police barracks, which was out of the question, he had done everything he could to see she was safe. After what she'd endured, the loss of her home during the attempt on her life, it set his teeth on edge to even think she might catch a bullet when he cranked it up on Paxson and company.

Bolan was about to break cover, dash across the gap between the mobile homes, when fate intervened to show him the way in. The man he'd used as a human shield at the motel crossed into his sight. The gunner looked over his shoulder, passed beneath the soft white light that burned from a lamppost, then kept marching. Bolan was up and running, mentally calculating the distance he would have to cover before he made his way up the far side of the last mobile home, ready to greet the man as he reached for the doorknob. It was just the guy's bad luck, he figured, that he would further Bolan's game plan. If he didn't want to go along with the soldier's program, his streak of bad fortune would come to a sudden end.

Swift and silent the soldier crossed over the gap to reach the targeted mobile home. He figured four, five men at best were inside, and was positive they would be armed, on high alert.

The Beretta leading the way, the Executioner picked up the pace as he hauled himself up the far side of the mobile home.

THE FACES OF FEAR that stared him back caused Hamilton to second-guess his role in the program. Before then he would have never even considered what he was now thinking. The ship was sinking, and it was time, he decided, to find a life raft before he went down right along with Paxson, drowning in the madness created by other men.

"Where's Paxson?"

"What's going on here?"

"Say something, damn it, man!"

Their buzz of questions swirled in his mind like an angry hornet's nest. What did they expect him to say or reveal? Sit tight, people, we're about to shoot you where you sit. All your work to create Godsbreath, much appreciated, but you've served the master who now sees you as an albatross. He chuckled at the little fantasized speech, and one of his men demanded to know what was so funny.

Funny? Death was never something to laugh about.

Hamilton found Tribble by his side, noted the worried look on the man's face.

"Two of them are missing."

Hamilton cursed. "There aren't many places they can hide. You have five minutes to find them."

The workforce smelled trouble, Hamilton knew, but in five minutes or so their worries would end. Hamilton walked out of the mess hall, found four of his men in the corridor. He took an extra HK MP-5 one of them had brought at his order, chambered the first round.

Hamilton could feel the panic rising beyond the doorway, felt a stab of bitter resentment that Paxson had left him to carry out this massacre. But he was a soldier, and his orders were explicit. Still, it was one thing to gun down an armed opponent, quite another matter altogether to murder civilians in cold blood, as if they were nothing more than sheep led to the slaughter.

Hamilton drew a deep breath through his nostrils, put some iron into his will, and told himself there was no other way but to march right in there in a few minutes and mow them down.

Beyond that, he admitted to himself he wasn't sure what he was going to do.

12

The targeted man opened the door, full attention riveted on the SUV parked on the hill at the edge of town, making him clearly suspicious. His back presented a perfect bull's-eye when Bolan made his charge. On a dead run, the Executioner rammed the MIB, propelling him through the doorway, a human missile sent flying into the mobile home to rudely announce Bolan's presence to whoever waited beyond. Inside, the Executioner found two more of Paxson's men jumping to their feet, subguns coming up, tracking on for the invader looming over their sprawled comrade.

Too little, too late, the shock and anger was wiped off their expressions in the next heartbeat.

The Executioner gave the Beretta a lightning double tap, drilling the men between the eyes with a 9 mm Parabellum round each. The thud of deadweight crashing to the floor was drowned by a sudden roar.

The gunner Bolan had shamed earlier was obviously hell-bent on winning this engagement. Before Bolan knew it, the man was up, whirling and grabbing the hand holding the Beretta. Bolan heard him snarling and cursing in his ear, the hardman surging into him, attempting to knock him down with sheer brute force. Bolan shifted his weight to the side, the gunner locking an arm around his back. They tussled toward the middle of the living room, then Bolan dipped at the knees, used the man's own angry momentum and flipped the gunner over his shoulder. The mobile home rocked as the man smashed a wooden coffee table into a pile of shards.

No sooner was Bolan stepping toward the gunner when the man lunged up, driving a shoulder into the soldier's gut. The Executioner was thrown back, shattering a mirror on the wall. The hardman flying toward Bolan was a blur, intent on caving in his face, but at the last instant Bolan ducked. The gunner drilled his fist through the flimsy wall. Sucking air into starved lungs, Bolan cranked it up a notch, waded in for the KO. The Executioner slammed the MIB a kidney punch and was rewarded by a guttural grunt of pain. The man was pulling his hand out of the wall when Bolan slashed a right off the MIB's jaw that whipped his head to the other side as if it were attached to a spring. A kick to the back of the man's knee, and Bolan sent him tumbling onto his back. The gunner searched out Bolan through a glassy stare, but before any sign of angry life could revive the man, the Executioner crouched and placed the Beretta's muzzle between his eyes.

"You have one hope," Bolan told the MIB.

"Kiss my ass."

"Not exactly what I wanted to hear. Last chance. Do you have a swipe card to get me into that compound?"

The MIB chuckled. "Sure. What, you want to just walk right in there?"

Bolan listened for any sound that would betray the presence of another man but heard only the rasping of the MIB's breathing. "That's the general idea."

"Why not? At least I'll get to watch you get shot to hell soon as you set foot inside."

"If that looks like the case, you'll be the first to go."

After learning his name, Bolan ordered Targon to roll over, but was forced to lend a rough hand getting the man on his stomach. A moment later, he bound Targon's hands with plastic cuffs and jacked him to his feet. Cautiously, expecting a subgun-wielding military man to come flying around the corner, Bolan manhandled his prisoner out the door.

He was about to question him about a key to the vehicle when he saw Sally Simpson rolling the SUV down the dirt road. A cloud of dust boiling in her wake, she jerked the SUV to a stop, hopped out and rasped, "I don't take rejection lightly, Belasko."

Bolan bit down a curse. He saw a few blinds pulled back from the mobile homes down the street, but the curious stayed put. It wouldn't matter what the temporary guests here did; Bolan was out of there.

"How come I'm getting the impression you're not going to listen so well?"

"If I wanted easy and pain free," she shot back, "I would have chosen another path in life."

Bolan clenched his jaw. "I suppose you'll follow me if I leave you here."

"I was under the impression you were calling in some sort of baby-sitting detail to pick me up and see me safely on my way."

Bolan marched the man around the corner of the mobile home.

"Where are you going?"

"To get my bag. Keep the engine running."

"So, I'm in?"

"Until I say otherwise," the Executioner growled over his shoulder.

"Fair enough."

"It damn well better be."

HAMILTON WAITED as long as he could, had even granted the hunting party an extra fifteen minutes. Now he passed the order to Tribble to keep searching, take care of the missing as soon as they were found. If the errant workers hoped to use their cards on the keypad to the front wall, sashay off into the desert, Hamilton already had a man stationed up top, poised to cut them down if they thought they could pull off another Randall.

"Let's do it," Hamilton told his four-man team of executioners.

He wondered why it had gone so strangely silent in the mess hall, entertained a paranoid notion the gathered sheep had sneaked out somehow, even though he knew there was no other way out but past him. He was rolling through the doorway, MP-5 up and ready to trigger off the first few rounds, when he suddenly found himself faced with a floodtide of human rage. They had broken under the strain of panic, their instinct for survival taking over in some burst of frenzy and chaos without any regard for the weapon he wielded, aware now they were dead men either way. So why stay put and take it? It would have been a tough chore, at best, gunning down thirty-plus men, hoping they would have stayed immobilized by shock and horror until the last few rounds were spent and their doom was sealed.

Before his mind could even fathom this display of insanity, Hamilton found himself forced to confront his own survival.

They wanted to die on their feet, Hamilton saw. So be it.

They were shouting and cursing, a din of pure rage so loud it pierced Hamilton's senses, balking him long enough for the human tornadoes to start blowing his way as they bounded from the Formica bench tops. Seeing hands clawed and poised to tear out his throat, he held back on the subgun's trigger. He mowed down the first wave, maybe a half-dozen or so white coats chopped up into crimson sieves, the stutter of four other SMGs in his ears, when the second wall of flesh descended over him.

"You bastards!"

"Think you can just murder us!"

"You're fucking dead, Hamilton!"

Hamilton kept firing point-blank into their mad charge. He felt the warm stickiness of blood hitting him in the face, glimpsed bodies dancing under the hail of lead scything into them, the red ruins of white coats dropping all around him. But with only five guns, now swarmed by an enraged mass of what he had once considered nothing more than meek and mild-mannered scientists, Hamilton knew the numbers alone would bowl them down within seconds. He cursed himself for waiting so long, giving them time to chew on their fear, working up the nerve to attempt this mass suicide charge.

The meek, he knew, were on the verge of inheriting the compound.

He went down under their pummeling fists, held back on the trigger even as he was falling, spraying bullets back and forth, riddling angry faces into pulpy mush. He felt the subgun ripped from his hands, feet banging off his head and face. The ceiling seemed to rain red as screaming, twitching forms collapsed on top of him.

A bitter thought took shape in his mind as he struggled to roll the red ruins of a corpse off his body, reaching for his Beretta.

Paxson would demote me if he could see this. Then the thought was kicked out of his head, as they vented their rage over this betrayal, threatening to drop him into a veil of blackness.

Driven by terror, he began firing wildly into the human stampede, the Beretta cracking off round after round, coring into skulls, stitching 9 mm Parabellum slugs into the spines of scientists rolling over executioners who became the executed in a few short moments. Subguns were quickly torn from the hands of the military men even as his men attempted to hold their ground, blaze away with the final few rounds. The lucky ones were beaten to death, their skulls kicked in, feet driving bone shards like spikes into their brains.

When the last MIB was sent flying out the doorway under the merciless barrage of subgun fire, Hamilton rose to a knee, triggering the Beretta as fast as he could. The mass exodus bulled out the doorway, bodies falling, arms flailing, Hamilton helping to launch a few scientists out into the corridor with several headshots. A howl of rage beside him, and he saw one man surging up from the sprawled bodies. Hamilton braced himself as the scientist hammered into him. He plunged the muzzle of the Beretta into the man's stomach, but the scientist bulldozed him to the floor. Three squeezes of the Beretta's trigger and Hamilton shoved the convulsing body away, started to stand, then slipped in the pooling blood beneath his feet.

Beyond the doorway he heard the weapons fire, the screams of men dying in agony, or the sound of bitter frustration that freedom wasn't in the cards.

Not for the scientists or Paxson's men.

Hamilton forged ahead, toward the siren call of hell.

BOLAN HAULED out Targon through the passenger door. While the soldier slipped into his combat harness, he checked the slope leading up the hill through his night-vision goggles. Beyond, on the other side, according to Simpson, was the ominous lair where Godsbreath was created. During the drive, Bolan put in the call to the Farm's blacksuits standing by with the jet. They were scrambled to both pick up the lady and, if Bolan came out the other side, two of them would hold down the fort until Brognola's HAZMAT team arrived.

"That was Paxson's jet we saw a few minutes ago," Targon said, sounding proud of something, but what, Bolan wasn't sure. "If you're going after him, you can kiss that idea goodbye."

True enough, Bolan had seen the dark speck streaking across the sky, heading in a southeast direction. If Paxson had bailed, he was currently en route for Dallas. Before following, Bolan had grim business to conclude here on this desolate stretch of Utah desert.

The architects of Godsbreath were about to be paid a call by the Executioner.

Bolan looked in the doorway, told the lady, "Stay put."

"I already heard you make the call."

"The jet will be flying in, fifteen minutes from now, give or take."

"Coming from Cedar City, right."

Bolan wasn't sure he cared for her tone, as if the lady were having second thoughts about staying put.

"You see it, hit your lights twice. No matter what happens, don't come looking for me. Are we clear?"

She nodded.

"If anyone shows up over that hill other than myself—"

"I'm to drive like hell away from here," she finished.

"You don't have to like it, Sally, just do it."

With his HK-33 in hand, Bolan nudged Targon. "Move out."

The man trudged ahead, leading Bolan up a rock-littered slope. The soldier watched the rise through the green tint of his goggles. There could be any number of motion sensors, infrared beams, hidden cameras monitoring Bolan's approach, tipping off the enemy. But if the lady was right, this was the hole in their security, and the fact that she'd not been rounded up during her own surveillance told Bolan the enemy had overlooked this particular stretch. Why the oversight didn't matter right then to the Executioner.

Bolan's goal here was pure and simple annihilation.

"You're crazy, you know," Targon said, "if you think you can just traipse in there and start blazing away."

"Get me in. I'll worry about the rest."

"If you…"

Bolan jabbed the military man in the spine with the muzzle of his assault rifle. "Enough talk. Keep walking."

They were topping out the rise when Bolan heard the sudden din of autofire, a scream lashing the air from below. Staring down, Bolan found the way into the compound was wide open, the maw in the side of the mountain lit up with enough light he was able to strip off his NVD goggles. Something had gone terribly wrong in the compound, with a full-scale slaughter under way. Two armed military men were just inside the opening, their subguns stuttering out long bursts that were kicking men in white coats off their feet, flinging them outside the entrance.

"Any guesses?" Bolan asked the man beside him.

"It's Paxson's final solution here. If it looked as if we were going to be raided or exposed, the order was to kill the workforce. Blow the place."

"Someone's funding this operation, and I'm thinking it's someone back east."

"Hamilton…"

"Who?"

"He's Paxson's second-in-command. He would know more about that than I would."

Bolan knew there was only one way he would find

any answers here, and beyond. He told Targon to describe Hamilton and the basic layout of the compound. When that was done, the Executioner filled the M-203 with a flash-stun grenade. He relieved Targon of his magnetic swipe card and got the three-digit code from the man, just in case they shut the door before he made it inside. It didn't look as if that was going to happen. Autofire kept rattling out the maw from some point just inside.

"Believe me when I tell you, this is going to hurt you more than me," the soldier said, and hammered the butt of the HK-33 across Targon's jaw.

When the hardman was down and out, the Executioner began his march down the slope.

13

"I can't say I like what I'm hearing, Major. Fact is, I've already heard the rumblings from several of my sources back here of the trouble you're having in Utah. It's out of control, and I'm thinking you're likewise out of control. We now risk exposure. Quite possibly, everything we've worked for, planned on, the hope for a New America is gone. Down the toilet—and because of one man? Is that what you're telling me?"

Paxson wasn't quite sure how to answer that one. A simple yes should have sufficed, but just saying "one man" would have left a sour taste in his mouth.

No matter what he said, he knew it was all going to hell, everything he was responsible for about to blow up in his face. He was sitting alone near the front in the cabin of his Gulfstream jet, with Kragen, Barber and Braxton in the rear. After his update—the hardest five minutes of his life—the long pauses on the other end fueled some paranoia he couldn't shake off. Right then he felt like the last man on earth, found himself wishing he could have been talking over the secured line from the moon. And Paxson clearly heard the bitter frustration in the general's voice, picked up on the man's fear, the edge in the tone that warned him the man was driven now to seek self-preservation.

And there he sat, saying the program may have to be scrapped simply because he couldn't take down one guy. In the dead of night, he'd left his men behind to clean up, and he was moving on for God only knew what. What about his own survival now? Well, the general may suspect he was chasing his own immediate future and safe haven, but he didn't know it was time Roger Paxson started looking out for number one.

Before he could bolt, drop out of sight, Paxson knew there were loose ends to tie up. First the Iranians, then maybe even the general himself if the man insisted on playing hard-ass, demanding an accounting for his failure.

Maybe money was all he needed, Paxson thought. He'd paid his dues, kicked ass for the Stars and Stripes, risked it all during the Gulf War. And for what?

Cold cash, yes, sir, to set himself up somewhere overseas. If he wanted to bail, why not go all the way? There were plenty of terrorist groups overseas who would pay a whopping sum for what he carried in the briefcase. Sell, sell, sell—that was the American way, wasn't it?

Then again, he might not make it out of America if he read the general's voice right, the accusation in the tone. The general would cover himself, the man all power and position, too much to lose, and he just might send a hunting party his way. If that happened, Paxson decided, and he found his back to the wall, Godsbreath could prove his last resort to save himself.

If he was left on his own, in the worst-case scenario he could blackmail an entire city, snatch up a fat ransom. Who was going to touch him, dare to get near him with what he had in his possession?

No one.

"What are you saying?"

"I'm saying," the general told him, "that if you have the material in question, you need to fly immediately to Washington. We'll meet in our usual room at the Key Bridge Marriott."

"A brief detour, then I'm on the way."

"Forget the Iranians. That was your little side job anyway. That wasn't part of why I brought you aboard. Are you forgetting that without me you wouldn't have had this opportunity?"

Paxson snorted. "You forgetting I'm one of those unsung Gulf War heroes, General, that you loved to boast so much about? You're talking to a guy who single-handedly kept the Israelis from turning Iraq into a glowing cinder."

"Your service to your country has been noted and much appreciated."

"You came to me. You had the dream."

"And you bought it."

"I did. But I'm not spending the rest of my life in Leavenworth."

A long pause. "I assumed you might head for Dallas. I'll have some men on hand. Let's just say they'll watch your back. As soon as you're finished with the Iranians, I'll expect you in Washington, no later than, let's say, five o'clock tomorrow evening. Will that be a problem for you?"

"I'll be there."

"Make sure you are. By the way, forget the meeting with the President and your grand announcement about a possible cure for AIDS."

The line went dead, leaving Paxson to ponder his future. So the general was sending in the watchdogs. Or were they black ops, going to Dallas to make sure the general's own backyard was cleaned up? Whatever. If shadows turned up on his tail, they were dead either way.

Paxson stood, moved to the rear. Grim-faced, he looked his men in the eye. "Gentlemen, listen up. We have to be prepared for a problem when we hit Dallas. I believe we just became a liability."

THE BLINDING WHITE LIGHT got the show started.

They were gagging, clutching their faces, staggering all around in the cloud of his flash-stun blast, when the Executioner rolled through the maw, tracking on with his assault rifle. Two of Paxson's men absorbed Bolan's first bursts of HK-33 autofire.

The Executioner was in the compound, charging through the boiling smoke of his surprise entry, the stink of death in his nose, but venturing down the corridor beside the elevator shaft presented his next challenge.

Crouching at the corner of the elevator shaft, Bolan took in the action as men in white coats streamed through what the soldier believed was the doorway to level one. Four levels, Targon had informed him, with the hot zone at the bottom. Bolan had come in, prepared to take it one level at a time, hunt the enemy down, flush them out, if necessary, with whatever it took, but Paxson's so-called final solution might just bring all concerned running straight into his gun sights.

Bolan waited until the first few white coats were nearly on top of him when he shouted, "Justice Department. Stop where you are."

"If you're Justice Department, I'm the President," a scientist growled, running but slowing his strides when he saw Bolan aim his weapon at the group.

"If I was one of them, you'd already be dead," Bolan replied.

"They just murdered a bunch of us," another white coat said, gasping for breath. The way in which the bald guy looked at Bolan, skidding to a halt, told the soldier he might have a believer on his hands. "Are you really from the Justice Department?"

"Outside, all of you," Bolan ordered. "Where's Hamilton?"

"Next level down," the bald scientist answered. "If he's even still alive."

"Clear this place. Help is on the way, but don't go too far," Bolan ordered. "You want to save yourselves, I'm your last and only hope."

They were running out of the compound when Bolan heard the clank and grind of the elevator car kick into motion. It was descending, picking up whoever was left below.

The Executioner checked the corridor beyond the open doorway to level one, found it empty down there. He wheeled around the corner, waiting in ambush for whoever was coming up.

With any luck at all, Bolan hoped Hamilton was moments away from walking right into his gun sights.

SHE HIT HER LIGHTS twice, as Belasko had instructed, when she saw the black jet soaring in from the direction of Cedar City. The jet banked, descended, flew in on a straight line, then finally touched down in the distance behind her. She was concentrating on the jet, knew the pilots had spotted her SUV, when she glimpsed the shadow in her side mirror—a heartbeat before her window caved in, shards tumbling into her lap, her startled cry lost in the cursing and shouting beyond her door.

He was like a fog, or a ghost in her eyes for a moment, then she recognized the face of rage outside her door as Belasko's prisoner. With his hands cuffed behind his back, she wondered how he'd smashed in her window, then glimpsed the dark streak of blood running down his forehead. A slew of questions wanted to burn through her mind—what happened, where was Belasko, was he alive or dead?—but the murderous intent in the eyes and the voice in the dark world beyond her SUV shocked her mind and body into what seemed an eternal paralysis.

"Get out, and get these cuffs off me, bitch! I know your boyfriend left something behind to cut me loose! Get out now or I'll kick this door in!"

The subgun. She touched it with trembling fingers, lifting the weapon, wondering if she could aim and squeeze the trigger, actually kill a man. Belasko made it sound easy. Aim low, since the weapon tended to rise.

"Your boyfriend's gone, honey! Big hero thought he could cold-cock me again and just go on about his business. You're on your own! Just you and me.

Come on, get out, I don't have the time for any of your shit!''

She scrambled over the passenger seat, almost dropped the subgun but somehow held on as he slammed more thunderous kicks into the door.

''Where you think you're going?''

She was outside, falling to the ground, the moment like some hazy dream as she plunged and hit the earth. The shadow rolled around the front, looming over her.

Could she do it?

''What, are you going to shoot me? I don't think you have the guts, honey.''

Laughter, harsh and ringing like distant bells in her ears. Aim low.

She did. He was lifting his leg back, to kick her in the face, when she squeezed the trigger. She heard the weapon stutter, rising, as Belasko told her it would, then heard the sharp cry of pain. Targon toppled to the ground, twitching like some fish out of water. Then the bile squirted up her throat, threatening to choke her. She let the vomit spew, emptying her guts as if the act itself was some cleansing of what she'd just done.

The world spun, the stars winking in and out in the mist of her vision. What seemed like an hour later, and she heard a voice, unlike the sound of fury she'd wiped out of her head with the killing of Targon.

''Ma'am, it's all right. We're with Belasko.''

HAMILTON.

They were rolling out of the elevator, five of Paxson's men all armed with subguns, including the one

Bolan's two-time hostage had described shooting him a startled look that betrayed his identity.

They were wheeling, lifting their SMGs, but Bolan beat them to the opening rounds.

A short precision burst from his assault rifle, and the soldier chopped off the lead gunner at the knees.

One down—Hamilton, he hoped—four to go.

Bolan armed a frag grenade as they hosed his position with subgun fire. It was risky, since he needed Hamilton alive, but he mentally marked off Hamilton's fall, hoped to give the second-in-command breathing room from the intended blast radius.

No choice but to chance it. The area around the maw was large enough to hold several 18-wheelers, enough room to maybe give Hamilton some hope that he wouldn't be ripped to shreds by shrapnel.

The raging hornet's nest of bullets swarmed the soldier's position, driving him to cover. They were shuffling ahead, spraying bullets, when the soldier whipped the steel egg around the corner, aiming for the maw, while still giving the men some lead.

"Grenade!"

The explosion sent one gunner flying out the hole, while two other hardmen screamed when the gale force of lethal steel fragments blew in their faces. The Executioner hit a knee, swung the assault rifle around the corner and mowed down the screamers with two short precision bursts of autofire.

One man fled for the desert.

Breaking cover, Bolan caught one of the group as he rose from the boiling smoke and cordite, the hardman's face looking like diced red onions. Bolan kicked him off his feet, marching a line of 5.56 mm lead across his chest. A voice, rife with pain, called out from the smoke.

"You...so, you're the guy has Paxson all shook up...wild man of the desert. Who the hell are you?"

"Not important."

"Yeah, I guess not. You are whoever you are. A wild man..."

Looming over the lone survivor, Bolan checked the man's injuries. He was bleeding fast and hard, and the soldier could only hope the man held on a few more moments. There was one man on the run. Only a clean sweep would satisfy Bolan.

"Are you Hamilton?"

"Yeah."

"Hang in there. I'll come back, we'll talk."

"Sure...why not." He choked out a bitter laugh. "This gig is dead anyway."

The Executioner left Hamilton to hold on. He ran through the maw, searched the rise and spotted his target climbing for the top. Bolan found the scientists, a huddled mass of fear in the dark shadows to his right.

"Sit tight, all of you."

"We're not going anywhere," one man yelled back.

"Just get us the hell out of here."

Bolan saw the exchange had alerted the man in black. There was no time to get locked into some long hunt for the guy. The Executioner loaded the M-203's breech with a 40 mm frag grenade.

The man started triggering his subgun, but he was stumbling uphill, in the dark, his rounds missing Bolan by yards, winging off the ground.

Bolan tapped the M-203's trigger, lit up the man's world a few seconds later, the man flying out of the smoky thunderclap, riding out of the blast to sail downhill, roll up in a broken heap.

Marching back to Hamilton, Bolan was greeted by another sound of strangled laughter. He wasn't sure what Hamilton found so amusing, but reckoned between the pain and the knowledge he was bleeding to death, linked with despair and bitterness that their warped dream was dead, had pushed the man to the edge.

"Paxson's plans?"

"Dallas. Going to wax the Iranians."

Hamilton paused and Bolan saw the light fading in his eyes as shock threatened to take the man down.

"Quickly."

"Beyond…if he makes it…Washington…Key Bridge Marriott…always meets the general there…"

"This general? I need a name."

"Pentagon brass…classified shit…CBW program… name's Crayton."

"Anyone else left alive here."

"Hell, no…just the two of us…don't leave me like this…I'm a soldier…Gulf War hero…"

Bolan nodded, grimly.

"One thing…black box in my pocket…we mined the place with plastic explosive…wouldn't want the wild man…of the desert to get blown up…by accident…you come this far…know what I mean…"

The Executioner gently took the box from Hamilton's pant pocket, then honored the man's last request.

WITH TWO of the Farm's blacksuits flanking him, the Executioner took a tour of the compound, striking level four off the circuit, content to leave the hot zone to the HAZMAT team. It was a basic compound, maybe tunneled in here by an army corps of engineers if this place of death was funded by black money. Who could say? It was all steel, floor to ceiling, two massive tunnel-boring machines on level three. Narrow corridors, conference and command-and-control rooms. He was searching for survivors but gave up as he took the elevator back to level two. The soldier stood in the doorway, giving the carnage a grim scrutiny. He wondered briefly who these men were, if they had even been aware of Paxson's ambitions. He supposed he could ask the scientists when he went back outside, but why bother.

There was Sally Simpson to check on. A blacksuit had informed him of what happened with the lady.

"I can't believe Paxson's men shot them like they were just diseased cattle, sir."

Bolan nodded. "It's finished here. You'll stay with the others until our people arrive."

Bolan walked for the elevator, anxious to leave.

Paxson was still on the loose, like some wounded animal out there, raging at the world. Bolan would catch up to him soon enough and put the man out of his misery.

"NOW WHAT?"

The soldier walked up to Sally Simpson. The lady was sitting on the ground, behind the jet. Bolan could tell she was clearly shaken up, a haunted look in her eyes that said she may never be able to forget having been forced to take another life.

"Are you going to be all right, Sally?"

"Just get me out of here. Yes, I'll be fine."

Bolan showed the lady a warm smile. "Words alone won't get you through it. But this will pass."

"I'm strong."

"I know."

"Maybe I should have listened to you. Maybe I should have just let you walk away."

"We get back to Washington…"

"Don't say it, at least not now, please. I can take care of myself."

"I was going to say if you need anything, just ask."

She looked up at Bolan, smiled. "Take me out to dinner and we'll call it even."

The lady was coming around. She would pull through this, put it behind her.

"Sounds like a plan."

"And I won't even ask a bunch of questions," she said, "about your life or who you really are."

Bolan gave the lady a wry smile. "That's good. Because if you did…"

She chuckled. "I know. You'd have to kill me."

The lady was a trouper. But any pleasant evening with Sally Simpson was on the backburner. There were traitors still to hunt down and send off to the eternal fire.

14

The Lincoln Continental had been waiting for him at Redbird Airport, as arranged, with the Iranians already contacted and in place for the rendezvous at the Holiday Inn. Dallas looked good for a clean sweep, then move on to D.C. and meet with the general, but a tractor trailer, dumped across I-35, had held Paxson back and seething for a good hour.

"Damn country," Paxson growled. "Freaking middle of the night. This has become a country of too many cars, too many people causing too many problems. Damn it!"

Finally his driver, Barber, rolled them past the state police barricade. Paxson checked his watch again, knew the Iranians were wondering where the hell he was, if he was even going to show.

"Are they still there?"

Barber glanced in his side mirror and nodded. "Black Ford, yes, sir, they just pulled out. Moving up on our six as we speak."

Paxson checked the load on his Beretta. He had four spare clips in his waistband. He looked at Kragen and Braxton. Plenty of backup with their two subguns, he figured. And the briefcase with Godsbreath was riding with him, all the way, no matter what, to be used as a last resort.

"The general's dogs? Or more Justice guys?" Kragen asked.

"We'll find out. Give us another mile ahead," Paxson told Barber. "Then pull it over and stop."

Barber maintained the speed limit while drivers who had been waved through the barricade shot past them in the fast lane. Paxson's next play might call unwanted attention, if some civic-minded citizen hit the panic button when he started dropping bodies all over the shoulder of the road, but he had no choice but to get the hellhounds off his back. Damn it, he raged to himself, in twenty-four hours a list of problems had grown so fast....

Don't think about it, he told himself. It was time to act, save himself. Starting now.

Barber slowed the Lincoln, swung off to the shoulder and parked.

"Kill the lights," the major ordered.

"Dropping in right behind us, sir," Barber said, when the headlights were shut down. "I'm counting four, Major."

"Gentlemen, watch my back. I'll handle this, but if it looks like things are going to get tight..."

"Understood, sir," Kragen said, cradling his subgun.

"You're covered, Major," Braxton said.

Paxson burst out the door on a surge of adrenaline, saw the four shadows disgorging from the Ford at almost the same instant, looking poised and ready to kick ass, unless he missed his guess. They were big goons, wearing black, and Paxson noted the bulges beneath their jackets, equally sure they could tell he was packing beneath his own coat.

"Did Crayton send you to hold my hand?"

"Do you know what you've done, Paxson, to the program?" the shadow by the front passenger door growled.

"The program's finished."

"If you have the product," the driver said, "hand it over now, and we can all be on our way."

"You're on your way, you got that right," Paxson rasped, and went for broke.

They were quick, he gave them that, their hands snaking inside their jackets, but Paxson had his Beretta out and cracking a 9 mm slug before they cleared leather. The driver absorbed Paxson's first round between the eyes, the slug coring through his brain, putting out the lights before he knew what hit him. Paxson was tracking on when he received a little help from Kragen and Braxton. He heard their subguns stuttering from behind, with Kragen a rolling blur in the corner of his eye as the man's MP-5 hosed the shadow behind the driver already plunging for the ground. What happened next was one of those moments of unforeseen chaos Paxson knew happened in every battle, large or small.

The shadows were falling, spinning under the hail of lead, when Kragen's target danced away from the Ford, stitched from crotch to sternum, and toppled to the highway. A pickup truck flew out of nowhere, its wheels rolling over the fallen shadow, bones snapping like pretzels, the body flailing several yards farther out into the road.

The driver of the pickup slammed on the brakes,

sending the vehicle into a long skid, tires squealing as tread clawed the asphalt. Paxson strode toward the pickup, saw two shadows and cursed the fact he had civilians to deal with now. A skinny figure with long hair slugged his way out the passenger door. Pumped on fear and adrenaline, Paxson stifled a burst of laughter when he saw he was facing down two crazy rednecks. Talk about bad luck, he thought, watching as a couple of empty beer cans clattered to the road, the skinny one drunk or high—and wielding a shotgun.

"What the hell's with you mother—?"

Paxson marched ahead, squeezing the Beretta's trigger, putting at least three rounds into the skinny guy's chest before he could finish his fit of cursing. The shotgun roared, emptied its load toward the sky as the skinny one dropped, hammered on his back. The driver was launching the pickup into gear when Paxson triggered the Beretta on the move, blowing in the back window with a storm of bullets. The satisfaction over seeing the driver's face slamming off the steering wheel was short-lived.

The skinny man was still breathing, choking on his own blood, telling Paxson he'd punched out a lung, as he loomed over the guy.

"Who...the hell...are you guys?"

Paxson sighted down the Beretta. "Gun-control nuts, that's who, you inbred. You look like something out of the sixties. I hated the sixties, it's where this country started to go to hell."

"Major, we have to go."

"Man, don't...don't do it," the man pleaded.

Paxson bared his teeth. "You know, gun control is being able to hit your target."

"I KNOW EXACTLY where it is. That's less than five minutes away, sir."

Bolan told his driver, Agent Chalmers, to make the Holiday Inn in three minutes, after he informed the man the location to where Paxson had been tailed. "Good work, Mathison," the soldier told the Fed on the other end of the cellular phone. "Don't make any move on the targets. Sit tight and wait." The order was confirmed and Bolan broke contact.

"I don't know how Brognola did it, sir," Chalmers said, flying the sedan down the airport freeway. "It's almost like the big man can just reach out, wave a wand and make it all happen. Damn near spooky, if you ask me. I mean, it's like Brognola could see Paxson flying into Redbird and made sure the other team was on-site to start shadowing the bad guys."

Bolan knew the truth, but the Justice agents Brognola had scrambled in Dallas had no clue about the existence of Stony Man Farm. And as far as they were concerned Bolan was simply Special Agent Belasko, his orders meant to be accepted without question, as if they were written in stone.

While Chalmers ate up the highway as fast as he could, Bolan suddenly felt the miles of this mission kicking in, but knew he'd suck it up, dig even deeper when he cornered Paxson. Indeed, Brognola, with cyber help from the Farm, had worked the usual magic. Redbird Airport, south of Dallas and just off the Marvin Love Freeway, was used by Paxson Pharmaceutical. It was no big secret, and it didn't take much effort for Kurtzman to hack into a few back doors over at the warehouse, iron out the logistics for the interception.

Cleanup was already under way. The HAZMAT team had secured the compound in Utah. Sally Simpson was on a red-eye flight with a blacksuit escort, heading back to Washington. No small blessings on those two scores, and Bolan was grateful that the lady was alive, with the lair of Godsbreath in the hands of the good guys.

Now it was just Bolan and Paxson.

The agent in charge of the watchdog Justice team had also informed Bolan that a few bodies were now sprawled across I-35. It didn't take much reasoning to conclude Paxson was out of control, and Bolan reckoned this General Crayton had sent a killing crew after the former Delta Force major.

The mystery Iranians were also now in the picture, if the late Hamilton had spilled the truth in his dying moment. Whatever their business with Paxson, well, Bolan intended to likewise shut them down. He could be sure Paxson wasn't selling the Iranians some wonder cure for the common cold.

"How do we play this, sir?"

Bolan was back in possession of the compact Ingram subgun, which was now snug in the special swivel rig beneath his windbreaker. He checked the clip, and said, "There's no 'we,' Chalmers."

"Sir?"

"You wait in the car."

"I don't understand, sir."

"You don't have to."

Bolan didn't feel inclined to explain Paxson was

walking around with perhaps the most lethal virus known to man. Too many players on the home team in his way, making Paxson any more jumpy than he'd already shown himself, and Bolan knew there was no telling what the man would do. Keep it simple. One man for the hunt.

The Executioner sat in hard silence. It felt as if it was soon to be a wrap, but he wasn't so sure. Anything could happen at the finish line.

PAXSON CHECKED the long hallway in both directions. Clear of human traffic. With the mess they'd left on the highway, he could feel the walls closing in even more, aware he needed this hit done, quick and clean. The sound suppressor was already threaded on the Beretta, and Kragen likewise had attached one to the modified muzzle of the MP-5 stowed in the small duffel bag. With Braxton and Barber outside in the parking lot, they were ordered to come running and shooting if a problem rolled in behind Paxson.

Paxson knocked on the door. He felt the fire burning inside, anxious to get the killing started. The door opened, and Paxson found the swarthy face of Rashid Takhti scowling back at him.

"You are late."

"We're here now," Paxson said, brushing past the Iranian. He counted four altogether, a big bruiser in silk threads standing by the window. Paxson had put them on the first floor, close to the lobby. No elevators, or steps, nothing but a quick evac once the deed was done.

Takhti shut the door. "This is most unusual. I hear

desperation in your voice, I fear something has gone wrong. We have paid half for the shipment...."

"Is that the money?" Paxson asked, nodding at the briefcase on the bed.

"Yes, but what about the shipment?"

Kragen knelt, unzipping the duffel bag.

"There's been a change of plans," Paxson said.

"I don't understand."

"You don't need to."

Paxson pulled the Beretta at the same moment Kragen hauled out the SMG.

"What the—?"

The first bullet that chugged from Paxson's Beretta drilled Takhti right between the eyes, turning the Iranian's expression of rage and confusion into a death mask.

CALL IT A FLUKE or some hand of cosmic justice guiding the way, but Bolan was so locked on to the scent of his quarry he sensed he could even feel the presence of Paxson in the building. It certainly aided Bolan's hunt when the deskman provided him with the room number, after the soldier flashed his Justice Department credentials, inquiring about three Mediterranean-looking men, armed with a vague description of Paxson and the hardman his Justice team had informed him had come into the lobby beside the ex-Delta major.

The Executioner intended to make some noise, bang on the door of the targeted room and take it from there.

It all went down in another direction—straight to hell, in fact—as Bolan found his enemies dropped in

his lap when he started to round the corner of the
first-floor hallway.

Paxson froze, startled for a split second at the sight
of the man who had caused him so much grief. He
was pulling out his Beretta but it was the subgun the
other hardman yanked out of the duffel bag that drove
. Bolan to cover behind the edge of the hallway's wall.
Autofire, muffled by the sound suppressor fixed to the
subgun, slashed the air above Bolan's head, slugs bit-
ing off plaster, whining off stone. Bolan brandished
the Ingram subgun, waiting for some lull in the enemy's fire to make his own move.

The soldier had been informed Paxson's two-man
backup team was in the parking lot, and Bolan's focus
strayed to the lobby doors. At the first sign of a problem, he figured the backup would come running.

They did.

The two from the car were flying through the doorway, their SMGs up and swinging when Bolan caught
them on the run, his Ingram stammering out a long
burst, the tracking line of death flaming across the
lobby. The Executioner sent them tumbling, a pair of
falling human brick walls, their legs folding beneath
them under the slugs chopping up their chests.

Bolan listened to the sudden silence down the hall,
peered around the corner, then heard the extended
chug of suppressed autofire. Bolting from cover, he
crouched at the doorway, wheeled and spotted Paxson
leaping through the blasted-out window.

The hardman covering Paxson held his ground by
the jagged shards of glass, hell-bent on aiding his
master's flight, and Bolan nailed the guy with a
figure-eight burst from his subgun. Crossing the room,

Bolan heard the shouting, the chugging of a sound-suppressed weapon, the cracking of pistols in the parking lot. He threw the curtain back and spotted Paxson shooting on the run, beating a hard flight across the parking lot. To keep the Justice team from being spotted by his quarry, Bolan had ordered them to stay put in the deep shadows at the far end of the lot, away from the Lincoln Continental.

It was a judgment call that opened the way for Paxson to reach the vehicle and attempt to bolt out of there.

Bolan squeezed between the glass teeth, dropped outside the window. Ingram up and tracking, he was giving chase when a voice from somewhere beside him bellowed, "Freeze! All of you! Drop the guns! DEA!"

They were streaming down the sidewalk, rushing him from the lobby. Bolan cursed as he watched the shadow that was Paxson hop behind the wheel of the Lincoln.

"I said to drop the goddamn guns!"

The three-man Justice team let the semiautomatic pistols slip from their hands and raised their arms.

"We're with the Justice Department," Bolan growled at the six figures with pistols drawn, the shadows closing.

Bolan dropped the Ingram, knew the DEA was one sudden move away from cutting loose. The soldier couldn't believe what was happening, cursed this slap in the face by fate. He could guess what had happened, not that it made any real difference to know the truth. The DEA had set up a sting here, heard the shooting. Now Paxson was fleeing, Bolan saw, driving out of the parking lot.

And the good guys were left stranded, faces smeared with egg.

The Executioner lifted his hands as the DEA swarmed him, fingers like steel talons snatching out the Beretta and Desert Eagle.

Bolan's grim laugh was flung back in his face by a voice snarling, "What the hell's so funny, tough guy?"

15

"My man said Paxson just left the bar," Brognola told Bolan after he hung up the cellular phone. "And my agent at the desk said Crayton and a guy the size of Godzilla just walked into the lobby."

The Executioner felt the adrenaline kick in. After the DEA snafu, seventeen hours were eaten up before Bolan now found himself in the passenger seat of the Chevy Caprice driven by Brognola. The big Fed had chewed ass off the DEA in Dallas before finally getting Bolan and his men untangled from their clutches. Critical time may have been lost, but the upshot was the Executioner's enemies had been tailed to the Key Bridge Marriott. Once again, the word of a dead man had panned out. While en route from Dallas to Reagan National, Bolan had suggested Brognola marshal all available resources to throw up a radar net around Washington and the surrounding suburbs. The big Fed had used his clout to get an AWACs in the air. Paxson's Gulfstream jet had been tracked to a private airfield in Leesburg, Virginia. There had been no time to rush any of Brognola's men to the airfield, but a few questions put to personnel at Paxson's Leesburg landing site, and the big Fed learned the ex-Delta Force major had cabbed it in to the Marriott.

"This guy, Paxson," Brognola said, rolling them into the parking lot, "has a serious death wish to just dump himself in our laps."

Bolan stared up the face of the hotel, the sun going down over I-66 beyond the Marriott, where the Washington workforce clogged the road in their daily struggle to get home. "He's living in fear."

"Of what?"

"Not being in control of the world."

"You have my full blessing to march up there and wax this guy."

Bolan nodded. "You've gotten me this far, I figure it's the least I can do."

And the big Fed scrambled once again to put the pieces into place. After Bolan shared with Brognola what he'd heard from Hamilton, the man from Justice planted two of his agents in the hotel. If Paxson was suspicious of any role-playing by Brognola's man at the desk and the agent acting as a bartender in the restaurant up top, the former Delta Force major hadn't shown the first hint of bad nerves.

"Paxson has the briefcase, Striker. That's my biggest worry. If he's cornered…"

"That's why I appreciate you letting me go up by myself."

"While I wait, sit on my hands and sweat it out?"

"It's the only call."

"Yeah, the Farm needs me more than you?"

"That's not exactly it. Just have your HAZMAT team ready to move on the double."

"They're already in place in the parking garage. Give the word, they'll be all over the room before you can blink twice." Brognola paused, then added,

"You know, these guys have some real stones. Paxson's been hanging out in the restaurant for two hours, nursing a cocktail like he's some tourist."

"Their own culture of arrogance will bring them down."

"By the way, I put Sally Simpson up in a hotel out in Fairfax. The way she asked about you, I gather she's also hoping you'll come out the other side on this."

"I promised the lady dinner."

"I'll have the tux ready when you come down. One last thing. Don't blow the whole room to hell," Brognola said, referring to the thimble-sized wad of plastic explosive Bolan would use to get him into the room. "The Department's budget for taking care of destruction of public property might be cleaned out on this one."

"A little dab should do it."

And the Executioner was out the door, on his way, leaving Brognola to ride it out.

PAXSON WAS STANDING by the window, staring at the Washington Monument down the Potomac River, thinking the whole town was a terrorist's smorgasbord of targets, when he heard the knock on the door.

"It's open, General."

He turned his head, saw the broad bulldog face, the general leading his bodyguard through the doorway. The guard shut the door, started reaching inside his jacket, Crayton staring at the briefcase on the bed, when Paxson growled, "I wouldn't do that if I was you. Not unless you want what's in that case to blow up, and in your face. I set the timer on one of the containers.''

They froze in midstride, the bodyguard pulling his hand back from the shoulder-holstered pistol. Paxson was lying, of course, but they didn't know that.

''You ever see someone die when they're struck down by that stuff? No?'' Paxson chuckled. ''I like this town when the sun's starting to set. Long shadows reaching over the river. The ants down there, fighting to get out to their little suburban enclaves. I was thinking about going up to the roof, and set off one those containers, just to see how many of them I can put out of their own misery.''

''You're insane, Paxson,'' Crayton said.

''No, I'm actually quite rational, General. I can see clearly now. When the going got a little rough, you wanted to cover your ass. Sent some of your flunkies to kill me, but I'm sure you already know they weren't up to the task.''

''The briefcase, then I'm gone.''

''You're already gone, General,'' Paxson said, and whipped out the Beretta.

THE EXECUTIONER HEARD the repeated soft chugging beyond the door, followed by cries of pain or outrage, he wasn't sure.

Didn't care.

They were going for broke inside, giving Bolan the element of surprise he needed to crash the party.

He was crouched, about to stick the plastic explosive to the doorknob when he tried the handle. The Beretta poised to lead his charge, he was twisting the knob when the door flew open and the foot lashed out, sending the weapon flying from his hand.

"You again!"

Bolan leaped up, reaching for the .44 Magnum Desert Eagle but saw Paxson whipping his face forward for a head butt. The soldier twisted his head, absorbed the blow off his forehead. It was enough force even still to explode a blinding white light in Bolan's eyes, rock his world, snap the life out of his legs.

"I'm going to do this the hard way since you insist on being a pain in my ass!"

He heard Paxson snarling and cursing, felt Paxson's hands digging into his jacket. Even as Bolan was pulled down, Paxson's foot spearing into his gut, the Executioner slashed a right off the man's jaw. There couldn't have been much behind the punch, because Bolan found himself flying through the doorway in the next instant. He hammered off the dresser, a mirror exploding into countless shards and slivers in the middle of his flight, arms windmilling as he launched off the piece of furniture and soared to some distant point across the room. The soldier hit the wall beneath the window, pain jarring him to the bone. Bolan was shaking the cobwebs out of his head, rising, when he heard Paxson bellow a curse.

"You're dead!"

And Bolan glimpsed Paxson running, then leaving his feet. The boots were aimed for Bolan's chest, the flying figure a blur in his starred gaze. The soldier wasn't sure how he reacted so fast, his bell rung, but pure instinct and reflex took over. Bolan dropped at the knees, thrust his open hands up. He made contact on Paxson's back, and the man's momentum did the rest.

The window blew out in giant shards. Bolan staggered back, watched as Paxson seemed suspended in midair, the man sailing out over the parking lot but hovering like some watching gargoyle.

"You fuuuuu..."

The curse followed the plunge, a shriek of rage they might have heard all the way to the White House. Bolan stepped up to the glass fangs, looked down as Paxson flipped and spun. A wet splat then reached Bolan's ears on the end of Paxson's dive. He half-expected the sprawled shape below to get up, but knew that was impossible.

The Executioner saw the dark stain pooling out from under the body and spotted Brognola's familiar bulk running, then standing over the corpse.

EPILOGUE

"We were too damn close to the edge on this one, Striker."

Bolan was standing beside Brognola on the Key Bridge walkway. The hotel had been evacuated by the Justice Department. Every law enforcement agency the Executioner could imagine—local, state and federal—now had the area around the Marriott cordoned off. The tenth floor was controlled by the HAZMAT team, who had taken possession of the briefcase with Godsbreath. News vans now jammed the streets of Rosslyn, with armies of reporters and cameramen being held back and barked at by cops and Feds at the edge of the hotel's lot.

Bolan turned away from the curious throngs, stared down the Potomac River as the lights of D.C. flared up against the encroaching night.

"To think if it weren't for Randall getting a conscience this thing would have turned into a nightmare unlike—"

Brognola abruptly went silent, appearing lost in grim thought. "You know, it shows me just how ill-prepared this country might be if some whackos with a few vials of even anthrax wanted to make some grandstand play. Tens, maybe even hundreds of thousands could be dead before we knew what the hell was out there killing them. I also have to wonder if there's any more black classified projects and compounds out in the desert. How many more Paxsons or Craytons are lurking around, thinking they're the only ones with the answers or want to make us all their slaves or blackmail us for money or whatever the bottom line here was?"

"We may never know."

"Unfortunately," Brognola said, "you're right about that. If anyone was involved at the Pentagon beyond Crayton, you can be sure if they're found out, they'll just deny everything."

"Seems to be the modern trend. Business as usual."

Brognola showed Bolan a weary smile. "Hey, don't go getting all cynical on me. Why don't you go get cleaned up? I thought you had a dinner date."

Bolan returned his friend's smile. It was good to put this one behind, he thought, and look forward to some quality time with a friend, brief as it might be, where life wasn't ugly, where at any second it could all be over.

"Go on, get out of here, Striker. Don't keep the lady waiting. Take the night and run with it, because we both have no idea what tomorrow will throw our way."

When all is lost, there's always the future...

JAMES AXLER

DEATHLANDS

THE SKYDARK CHRONICLES
Book III

Shadow Fortress

The Marshall Islands are now the kingdom of the grotesque Lord Baron Kinnison. Here in this world of slavery and brutality, the companions have fought a fierce war for survival, on land and sea—yet the crafty baron still conspires to destroy these interlopers. They cunningly escape to the neighboring pirate-ruled Forbidden Island, with the baron's sec men in hot pursuit...and become trapped in a war for total supremacy of this water world.

Available in September 2001 at your favorite retail outlet.

James Axler

OUTLANDERS®

SARGASSO PLUNDER

An enforcer turned renegade, Kane and his group
learn of a mother lode of tech hidden deep within
the ocean of the western territories, a place once
known as Seattle. The booty is luring tech traders and
gangs, but Kane and Grant dare to infiltrate the
salvage operation, knowing that getting in is a life-
and-death risk....

In the Outlands, the shocking truth
is humanity's last hope.